ROMANCING MISS FITZGERALD

A SAPPHIC AGE GAP ROMANCE IN THE 1940S

AVEN BLAIR

CONTENTS

Copyright Page

CHAPTER 1

HELENA

Savannah Georgia
The Savannah Grand Hotel
November 1949

As I sit in the lounge of The Savannah Grand Hotel with Alex Carrington, a former model who once worked with Victor Voss, I'm simply captivated. Her charm is a blend of wit, warmth, and playfulness all wrapped in an alluring and elegant presence. It's hard not to be drawn to her, and I find myself completely intrigued and attracted to her.

"I can't believe I've just bumped into you here in Savannah, Helena! I hope Miss Lomax didn't leave because of me," Alex says, her voice filled with a mix of surprise and concern.

"Oh, don't worry about that," I say, catching her gaze. "I flew to Savannah to meet with Laura and finalize the contract for Lomax Inc.'s photography services for Victor Voss over the next two years." As I speak, I'm captivated by the warmth in Alex's midnight eyes, their depth and allure drawing me in. "Laura and I will wrap things up tomorrow," I add, smiling back at Alex.

Alex gives me a warm smile and replies, "That means I can keep you to myself this evening."

My heart expands and thumps at her willingness to spend the evening with me. I take a moment to enjoy her excitement, sipping on my wine as I continue to gaze into her midnight eyes.

"I'd love to spend the evening with you, Alex," I say enthusiastically. She gives me a playful grin and then nods. "Would you like to have dinner with me?" I ask, my gaze never leaving her captivating dark eyes.

"Of course," she replies quickly.

Glancing at my watch, I say, "It's only 6 o'clock. Would you like to meet in the restaurant at about 7:30 or perhaps go out somewhere?"

Alex takes a sip of her wine and then says, "How about we meet in the restaurant? I'm not really in the mood to go out. Is that alright with you?"

Nodding, I say, "Of course. Let me go to my room and relax a bit, then change clothes, and I'll meet you at 7:30, okay?"

"That sounds lovely Helena. It still feels unreal that I bumped into you here in Savannah," Alex says, her tone softening with a hint of flirtatious playfulness. "I've always been very fond of you. I'm not sure if you were ever aware of that."

Flattered by her comment, I hold her gaze and softly reply, "No, I wasn't aware of that, Alex, but it makes me happy to hear. Many of the models thought I could be strict and demanding."

"You were!" Alex exclaims, then bursts into a bright laugh. With a playful glint in her eye, she adds, "But that only made you sexier to me, Helena Fitzgerald." She winks, her voice dropping to a soft, teasing tone.

My heart fills with butterflies that take flight and lunge downward, flooding my feminine essence with a throbbing ache. Oh god, what a rush, what is she trying to do to me? With a grin, I say, "Well, you're the first model who has ever told me I was sexy, Alex. Thank you for the compliment."

Alex keeps a playful grin on her face as she says, "I'm sure I wasn't the only one who thought so, Helena. I mean, you're incredibly gorgeous with that blonde hair and those steel-blue eyes. They just didn't have the guts to tell you that you were—and still are—very sexy, Miss Fitzgerald."

Smiling at her, I know she's genuine, but she's also enjoying watching my reaction to her flattery. I lean in with a grin and reply, "Well, I remember how gorgeous you were even back then, Alex. I hated it when you left us, I truly missed you."

Tilting her head a bit, she asks, "You did?"

Taking another sip of champagne, I keep my eyes on her and reply, "Very much. Why does that surprise you, Alex?" I ask as I keep command of her midnight eyes that just sparkled brightly at my remark.

Alex's mood seems to shift, and she softly says, "I guess I didn't feel like I would be missed if I left." She looks at me, a bit shocked, and adds, "I loved working with you, but I never expected to be missed, just simply replaced."

"Replaced!?" I exclaim with dismay, shaking my head. I reach for her hand, my fingers brushing against hers as I smile into the depths of her dark, midnight eyes. "No one replaced you, Alex. That would be impossible. Yes, we hired another model, but you... you were irreplaceable, darling."

Alex looks almost stunned as our fingers delicately inter-twine, and then I see her eyes glisten. Smiling at her, I softly ask, "Are you okay, Alex?"

She nods, her expression softening as a touch of somber-ness lingers in her eyes. Leaning closer to Alex, I softly whisper, "Why don't we go to my room and order a bottle of champagne."

Alex's lips curve into a warm smile as those midnight eyes lock with mine. Her voice is faint, yet it sends a ripple through me. "Helena, your eyes... they're so chilling, yet incredibly warm."

I smile in return, my heart skipping a beat at her words. Then, with a slow, deliberate nod, she adds, "I would enjoy accompanying you to your room very much, and I love champagne."

On the elevator, Alex says, "I'm sorry I got so somber, Helena. That was such a sweet statement you made; it touched me."

Reaching for her hand, our fingers intertwine once again. Making our way into my hotel suite Alex says, "You mentioned that you needed to rest before dinner. Perhaps I should go to my room and meet you later."

"Come here, Alex," I say as I give her a demanding look. She doesn't move, so I approach her, take her in my arms, and hold her.

"Pulling her tightly, I reply, "Thank you, Alex, for being so honest about how you felt about me." As I hold her close, I thread my fingers through her raven hair and add, "You've grown into such a beautiful and amazing woman, Alex. I'm so happy you're here."

Alex gazes into my eyes and softly replies, "I meant every word I said, Helena. You were and still are a very gorgeous and sexy woman."

As we stay in this tender moment, I glance at her full lips and know how much I would enjoy kissing them. Looking back to her eyes, I say, "Let me order that champagne, Alex." Do you have a preference?" I ask as I release her.

"How about Moët & Chandon? I like their Brut Impérial.

Does that sound good to you?" She asks as I walk toward the phone.

"Of course, that's an excellent choice; let me call them now."

As I wait for room service to pick up, I stand and look at Alex. I can't get past her dark raven hair and midnight eyes. But my gaze travels down her lovely body, enjoying every curve and lingers to her feminine essence. She glances over her shoulder at me as my eyes are on her lovely ass.

She immediately giggles and gives me a charming grin. I know I'm caught, so I decide not to play it off. Instead, I wink slowly, admitting that my eyes were roving over her feminine landscape.

After I order the champagne, I walk toward her with a grin. "They said it'll be up shortly."

Alex smiles, her eyes sparkling with an idea. "After champagne, why don't we go to my suite for dinner? I'll order room service for us," she suggests, her voice soft and inviting.

Feeling the warmth of her presence, I reply, "That sounds lovely. Then I won't have to miss you between champagne and dinner."

Alex gives me a faint laugh and then reaches around me playfully. "What a sweet thing to say."

Catching her hand, I gently pull her toward the sofa. Wrapping my arm around her waist, I reply, "I meant every word, Alex." The warmth between us lingers, and I want to remain in this moment a little longer.

Reluctantly releasing her, I say, "Have a seat, Alex." As she sits on the sofa, her dark eyes remain on mine. Sitting beside her, I gaze at her and then say, "Tell me why you're here in Savannah and all about your life, Alex. It's been seven years since we've seen one another, so I'm sure you have a lot to tell me about your life."

Alex gives me what seems like a nervous laugh, then says,

"Perhaps I need some champagne in me to be completely open about my rollercoaster life since you last saw me."

"Well, I understand. Hell, we might need two bottles for me to open up about my trials and tribulations." Alex responds with the same bright laugh she gave me earlier in the lounge.

As we both chuckle, we hear a soft knock on the door, "Oh, that must be our champagne, and just in time," I say as I laugh all the way to the door.

Letting the concierge in, he kindly opens the champagne and pours two flutes, then places the bottle back in the ice bucket. After he leaves, I walk toward Alex, whose gaze hasn't left me, hand her a glass, and sit beside her.

"Well, my dear. What shall we toast to?"

"Hmmm, I don't know, Helena. Why don't you make it for us," she says sweetly.

As I try to gather my thoughts, I see Alex's dark eyes gazing at me. Turning to her, I say, "You mentioned my eyes earlier, so now I want to toast to your exquisite midnight eyes. They could surely break the hearts of kings and queens alike."

CHAPTER 2

ALEX

Touching my flute against Helena's, I say, "My goodness, Helena, I had no idea you could be this charming. Thank you, that's a very delightful and enchanting toast."

"I meant every word of it, Alex," I reply softly as I gaze at her.

After our first sip of champagne, we settle into the sofa to get more comfortable. "Okay, you've had a sip of champagne, so why don't you tell me a bit about what you've been up to all these years, Alex."

I feel the same familiar dread whenever anyone asks me this question. I'm even more anxious now, but I will give her my usual speech. Helena is very special and deserves more, but this is how it has to be for now.

Taking another sip, I look at her and say, "Well, over the past few years, I've worked in public relations with an agency. It was a demanding role that involved a lot of client interaction and high-profile events. It's been an intense but valuable experience. Now, I'm focusing on transitioning into something I've always been passionate about—launching my own jewelry line."

"Alex! That's wonderful! Your own jewelry line? That's amazing, how long have you been working on this?"

"Over the past year. That's why I'm in Savannah, to source Aquamarines for my signature pieces. I actually have some sketches in my room that I'd love to show you when we go up, if you'd like to see them."

"Of course, I'd love looking at them!" Helena says with an excited tone.

"I'd love to share them with you, Helena. I don't show them often, but you're incredibly special to me. Plus, I want your opinion as a woman and art director."

"I can't wait to see them, Alex. We might have to take this bottle up now!" Helena says with excitement.

"You've always been so kind to me, Helena. They'll keep until dinner; they aren't going anywhere. I'm pleased that you want to look at them; that makes me incredibly happy."

"Oh, hush! I can't wait to see them, love," she exclaims. Then adds, "Tell me about the public relations career you've had. " Helena gazes at me in anticipation.

Taking a sip of champagne, I tell her, "My public relations work involved managing events and handling various client needs. It was busy and often unpredictable, but I enjoyed the challenge of making everything come together smoothly."

"Well, it sounds like it was indeed challenging, and with that background, it will help you in your new venture. Do you have a name for your Jewelry business, Alex?"

"I'm calling it *The Alex Collection.* I want to specialize in gold and silver bracelets, to begin with, and perhaps brooches."

Helena gracefully crosses her legs and drapes her arm across the back of the sofa, effortlessly entering my personal space. It immediately gives me butterflies that take flight straight across my heart. "Alex, I love that idea. Specializing in one area is a very smart business move. So many people go too broad, which only dilutes their brand and confuses clients and customers. I can't wait to see these designs."

"Thank you, Helena. That means so much to me. You've always been a smart businesswoman, and Victor Voss is lucky to have you."

Helena reaches for my hair and twirls her fingers through my loose locks of curls, giving me a sweet smile, but I see something more profound. "Would you like some more champagne, Alex?"

Seduced by her touch, I glance at my champagne glass and quickly say, "Yes, please." As Helena stands to refill our flutes, I take this opportunity to admire her. My gaze lingers on her shapely hips, perfectly accentuated by her skirt. With her jacket discarded when we arrived in her room, the sheerness of her silk blouse allows me tantalizing glimpses of her silhouette, subtly revealing the contours of her womanly figure.

As Helena hands me my champagne, I ask, "So, where are you with Victor Voss? You should own the company by now because I know you run the place."

Laughing, she says, "You're giving me way too much credit, my dear, but two months ago, I was promoted, so now I'm the CCO, Chief Creative Officer."

"Helena!" I Exclaim, then leap over and grab her, giving her a warm hug. Then I add, "That's wonderful; I'm so happy for you."

Helena pulls me to her and softly says, "Thank you, Alex. That's very kind." I can't help but smell her intoxicating aroma, Chanel, no doubt, but Helena's body scent seems to have given it its own unique depth and complexity, rendering me unable to pull away from her, so I don't. And neither does she.

As Helena holds me in her arms, I want to simply submit to her. How or why, I don't know. There's just something about this woman that has always moved me, and even more so now that I'm older and can appreciate her sensual maturity.

Moving closer, I softly say, "You feel so good, Helena." She doesn't say anything; she just pulls me closer, and I grin. Threading my fingers through her soft blonde hair, I whisper, "Your smell is intoxicating."

Helena giggles and asks, "Is this champagne getting to you, love?"

"Most likely. How about you?" I ask playfully.

Helena moans, and says, "It definitely is, but mixed with your allure, Alex. I'm completely hypnotized."

"And you have me completely spellbound, Miss Fitzgerald."

"I do?" She asks softly.

"You know you do, Helena. And you also know I had a terrible crush on you seven years ago, don't you?"

Helena pulls away gently but remains close as she threads her fingers through my hair. Gazing into my eyes, she replies, "I don't know, Alex. Maybe I did, but my life was so wrapped up in Victor Voss that's all I could see. But, love, I definitely noticed you."

Pulling back, I say, "I know your whole life was Victor Voss, Helena. May I ask you something?"

"Of course, Alex," she replies softly, tucking a few strands of hair behind my ear.

Taking a sip of champagne, I glance out the window and pause for a moment. Feeling Helena's eyes on me, I turn back to her and take another sip. Helena holds my hand and glass to prohibit me from taking another sip. "Ask me anything, Alex."

Clearing my throat, I gaze into her steel-blue eyes and ask

boldly, "Does Victor Voss still demand so much of your time that dating would be impossible for you?"

Helena touches my cheek, grins, and softly says, "Alex, I live in Chicago, love. How could we make that work?"

After she releases my hand, I immediately take a sip of champagne and reply, "I don't have a clue, Helena. Do you?"

Her head begins to nod, and I let out a nervous sigh, feeling as though I've just been rejected. But then Helena takes my flute, sets it on the sofa beside hers, gazes at my lips, and softly says, "I've wanted to kiss your perfect lips since you walked into the lounge, Alex. May I?"

My heart races, and I feel anxious excitement and an aching desire for her. I barely manage to whisper, "Yes, you may."

Helena cups my cheek and gently caresses my jaw with her thumb, her eyes fixed on my lips. She pulls me in, and when our lips meet, her kiss is so tender it seems to dissolve everything else, leaving only the softness between us.

My hand slides to the back of her neck, gently pulling her closer, and I return her kiss with the same delicate touch. There's no rush; it feels as though time has paused, allowing us this quiet moment to simply love each other.

Parting our lips, I feel Helena's warm tongue brush against mine with the same tenderness our lips delighted in. Our tongues have chosen the same rhythm and gentleness. I'm so completely lost in this woman and could stay in this moment, this room with her all night without one regret.

Helena breaks our kiss and whispers, "Those are the sweetest lips I've ever kissed, Alex." Then she leans back against the sofa, pulling me to her. Then she adds, " Thank you; that was magical."

"Thank you? Miss Fitzgerald, there's no need to thank me. My lips reveled in the pure delight of your tender touch," she softly replies.

As Helena holds me she gently asks, "Alex, how old are you, love?"

"Old enough, Helena," I reply with a chuckle as I grin at her. Then add, "I'm 32, Helena."

Helena gazes at me and nods, remaining silent for a moment before softly saying, "Alex, I want you to know I'm 52 years old. That's quite an age gap between us, love. Does it bother you?"

Leaning in, I kiss her lips tenderly, and reply, "Helena, all I see when I gaze at you is a desirable, passionate, and mature woman that I've thought about for years. So no, sweetheart." Threading my fingers through her hair, I add, "In fact, I find your maturity incredibly seductive and alluring. It makes me weak sometimes. I should be embarrassed to admit that, but I'm not.

Pulling me close, she whispers, "Well, I must confess, Alex, your youthfulness is quite alluring. I find you utterly charming and incredibly enticing, my love."

Taking our champagne, Helena hands me mine, grinning as she winks at me. "Well, Helena, I'm going to my room to order our dinner. Why don't you take time to change if you'd like and then join me when you're ready?"

Brushing against my hair, she says, "I'd love that.

Helena stands and reaches out for me. I rise, pulling her close, and we both laugh nervously. She softly says, "I'll see you soon," and then gently kisses my lips again.

Back in my room, I immediately walk into the bathroom and gaze at myself quietly. Tears start to well up in my eyes. Grasping the edge of the sink tightly, I let out a frustrated cry while looking at my reflection.

"You don't deserve her, especially when she finds out what you are," I think. Grabbing a tissue, I dab at my eyes, but my mind keeps churning with harsh thoughts. *"Public relations?! Really?!*

Those are fancy words for what you are. Yes, you did handle your client's needs," my mind mocks me.

Finally, I say aloud, "Shut up! I want this woman, and I've started a new life with my exclusive jewelry line. She admires that; and that's all she needs to know!"

Touching up my makeup and adjusting my hair, I look at myself in the mirror and smile gently, accepting that I'm not perfect but a good and honest person. I know I have to tell Helena, but I'll wait until the moment is right.

Changing clothes quickly, I head to the phone to call room service and order a very special dinner. As I pick up the receiver, I'm overcome with anxious excitement. Closing my eyes, I smile and think, *"I can't believe I'm having dinner with Helena Fitzgerald, and she kissed me so tenderly just moments ago."*

CHAPTER 3

HELENA

C hanging into a pair of high-waisted tailored trousers and a silk blouse, I can't help but smile, though I wonder why this captivating woman is so interested in someone my age. She's a goddess; she could have anyone she wanted. *Why me?* I think to myself.

Checking my hair and makeup, I flip off the bathroom light and smile all the way to the door. As I enter the elevator, the door closes, and a wave of nervousness hits me. I haven't been with anyone in years, and never someone so young.

When the elevator doors open, I pause for a moment. Suddenly, I think about the kiss, Alex's delicate lips against mine. With a deep breath, I hold my head high and smile as I gently knock at her door.

Alex opens the door with a charming smile, "Come in, Helena."

After she closes the door, I whisper, "I missed you." Alex gives me a nervous chuckle, which warms me. You look even more beautiful than when I left you only moments ago. How is that possible, Alex?" I ask as I touch her cheek.

She pulls me close and replies, "And you look even more ravishing, Helena." She takes my hand and says, "Come on, our dinner is waiting."

Walking into Alex's suite, I'm overwhelmed by the sight of a beautifully candlelit table adorned with fresh flowers, wine, and what appears to be fine china plates and crystal goblets. "My gosh, how did you manage to set all this up so beautifully in..." I pause to check my watch, then add, "in just thirty-five minutes?"

"Well, I had some help from the staff. You see, I simply bribed them to get all of this set up in twenty minutes," she replies as she laughs and intertwines her fingers with mine. Then she adds, "Come on, let's eat."

Alex holds my chair as I sit, "Thank you, Alex. I feel I should stand and hold your chair, my love."

"Helena, you are my guest, so please stay seated."

Smiling at her and completely enchanted, I whisper, "Thank you for this." I shake my head and grin.

"What are you grinning at?"

"You, Alex. Had I known you were this romantic and chivalrous, I would have paid more attention to the crush you mentioned and spent less time focused on Victor Voss, my love."

She beams at my comment. "That's very kind, Helena, but I doubt that twenty-five-year-old Alex would have been able to hold your attention."

"I somehow doubt that, Alex. When I told you I missed you, I was very sincere. The sadness I felt surprised me, revealing the void you left behind."

"Helena, that's so very kind, and it pleases me that you missed me because I truly missed you," I say softly.

"I know we already had champagne, but I ordered a bottle of wine. Hopefully, with some food in me, I won't act so silly," Alex chuckles.

"Alex, I didn't find you silly at all, love. I found you quite delightful with a bit of champagne in you. I think I'll order a case and keep it on hand," I say, grinning.

"But Miss Fitzgerald, I didn't think you had time to date me. Why would you need a whole case of champagne?" she asks playfully.

I place my silverware gently on the china plate, gaze across at her, and see the candlelight reflecting in her midnight eyes. "Let me tell you something, Miss Carrington —I will make the time. I'd be a damn fool to let you slip away."

A broad smile spreads across Alex's face as she responds, "Good, because I wasn't going to let you go regardless. I'm not finished with you, Helena. Not by far," she says sternly with an intense gaze.

When I wake the following day, soft light floods the room. Immediately, my thoughts drift to Alex. I glance at the clock on the nightstand and see that it's 7:35. She's most likely on her flight back to Chattanooga.

Last evening with her was amazing. We talked for hours after dinner about everything between several intimate kisses. Grabbing the spare pillow, I hug it and smile as I'm overcome with her tender essence. This woman truly makes me happy. I don't know how in the hell we will make it work, but I'm going to try. I love Victor Voss, but that company isn't going to continue to rob me of romantic love as it has done for years.

As I lay and think about how genuine and beautiful she is, I can't help but feel as though she is keeping something from me. She was very open about her feelings about me, but there is something else.

Pushing myself out of bed, I stretch thoroughly before heading to the shower to start my day. I have to call Laura to finalize the contract, and my plane back to Chicago leaves at 2 o'clock.

When she picks up, I hear, "Hello, this is Laura Lomax."

"Good morning, Laura Lomax. How are you and that lovely goddess of yours today?"

Laura bursts into laughter. "Something tells me you've got your own goddess now, so hands off mine!"

Chuckling, I reply, "You know I just tease you about Erin to *get your goat*!"

"*Get my goat?!*" Laura laughs harder. "I haven't heard that in years—my grandmother used to say that."

"Well, mine did, too. It must be a generational thing. Do you want to meet for lunch around 11 o'clock, if you can?"

"Sure, I can meet you then. I have an outdoor shoot at 3:00. What time is your flight?"

"It's 2 o'clock."

"Great, that will give us plenty of time for you to tell me all about that gorgeous woman that I know you spent the night with."

"No, I didn't."

"You didn't? Helena, that woman is crazy about you. Why not?"

I go silent for a moment as my feelings for Alex swim through my veins and then gently land softly on my heart.

"Helena?" Laura says softly.

Clearing my throat, I say, "I'm here, Laura."

"Are you okay, honey?" She asks, concerned.

"Yes, I'm fine, Laura. No, I didn't sleep with her because I was too scared to, and I believe she was as well."

"Okay, Helena. Look, you get yourself packed, and I'll pick you up at 11, and we'll have lunch, then I'll take you to the airport. I'm bringing Mark, and he can return your rental car. Is that okay?"

"Thank you, Laura, you're such a good friend to me," I reply softly.

Hanging up the phone, I begin to cry and don't fully understand why. Then I finally realize and it hits me hard. I sit on the couch and realize without a doubt that I already miss Alex and know what she has done to me.

Laura and I walk into *Old Towne Café* and settle into a booth by the window. It's just past 11, so the place isn't too crowded yet.

"Laura, thank you for picking me up and having Mark return my rental car. You don't realize how much this has helped me."

"Oh, hush, Helena. I'm your friend—that's what we do, we look after each other."

Shaking my head, I smile. "Yes, we do, honey."

As we order lunch, I sip my coffee, falling into a quiet reflection. Laura waits patiently; it's clear that last night with Alex has left me feeling off balance.

Finally, Laura breaks the silence. "What do you feel for her, Helena?"

Gazing into my friend's eyes, I softly reply, "Everything, Laura. I feel everything."

"Oh, Helena, I've never seen you like this. I don't know if I should be happy or sad. I am happy that a wonderful woman has turned your head, but you seem so subdued. Why, honey?"

I feel the tears. As I catch them with my napkin, Laura reaches for my hand and holds it tenderly. "Last night, it was as if Pandora opened her box inside my heart, and now it will never be the same again." Laura squeezes my hand to comfort me. Then she sits beside me and places her arm around me.

Laura whispers, "Why isn't that a good thing, Helena?"

"She lives outside of Chattanooga, and I'm in Chicago or always on the road. How is this ever going to work?" I ask as I weep a bit more. Then I add, "I shouldn't have asked her to my room last night; that was foolish."

"Do you really regret that, Helena," Laura asks softly.

Nodding, I reply, "Not one bit. Alex is simply amazing, Laura."

Laura kisses my cheek, then returns to her seat across from me, her gaze warm and smiling. As I start to laugh through my tears, I shake my head and grin at her.

"So you didn't sleep with her, Helena?"

Nodding, I reply, "Thankfully not. But a big part of me regrets it. I mean, I'm torn—damned if I had slept with Alex and damned that I didn't get to know her intimately. I can't even imagine how beautiful that would have been."

Laura and I had a good talk, and we signed the contract. Now, I'm on the airliner awaiting takeoff. A very pretty stewardess approaches me with an envelope in her hand. "Hello, are you Miss Fitzgerald?"

Surprised, I reply, "Yes, I'm Helena Fitzgerald."

Smiling at me, she says, "I have this envelope given to me by one of the porters. He said a young woman left it with him early this morning. She asked him to please make sure you received it."

Reaching for the letter, I feel Alex's essence move through me like the softness of the early morning light. "Thank you," I say almost breathlessly.

Holding it gently, I feel the plane begin to move forward.

Glancing out my window, I watch in a fixed gaze as the airliner leaves the runway. Below me lies Savannah, the city where last night I lost my heart to Alex Carrington, and the memories come flooding back.

Opening the letter I smell it, and the aroma is her, it's Alex. I smell her in all of her complexity and mystery I've yet to uncover. Unfolding it delicately, I see it's a short note, and I begin to read her lovely words:

My Dearest Helena,

Last night with you was nothing short of magical, a perfect prelude to something truly enchanting. Saying goodbye to you was pure torment. You're so rare and special that I chose to hold back on pursuing you intimately, believing that a bit of patience will yield its own beautiful rewards.

You have no idea how delighted I was when you invited me to your room for champagne. Though I struggled to express it last night, my feelings for you have long exceeded a mere crush. So here I am, confessing it all:

I, Alex Carrington, admit I was utterly love-struck by Helena Fitzgerald at just 25

years old. I cherished every moment I could steal a glance at her, captivated by her radiant presence.

Now, at 32, I'm even more enchanted. Last night, I was swept away by your beauty, intoxicating scent, and your kind and tender heart. Each kiss left me longing for more, completely lost in your depths.

This note serves as a reminder: I'm not done with you, Miss Fitzgerald. Any thoughts of slipping away are best forgotten because I will pursue you wherever you try to hide.

So it's best if you simply *toss up your white flag* and surrender to me willingly.

Yours always,
Alex Carrington

After reading her letter, I turn toward the window and smile the widest smile I've known in years. My goodness, what a letter from this incredible woman who clearly has no intention of letting me go. I chuckle as I reread her wit, humor, and tenderness, all intertwined in this lovely note. Folding the letter, I hold it to my face, breathing in her aroma again. I smell my darling Alex and feel her presence in my spirit and heart.

CHAPTER 4

ALEX

A smile spreads across my face as I pull up to my farmhouse just outside of Chattanooga in my MG Roadster. Something about driving up to this place never fails to lift my spirits. My grandparents left it to me a few years ago, though I've only called it home for the past six months.

The farmhouse needed a lot of work, but I've done my best to preserve its original charm. As I jump from the roadster and step onto the front porch, I still half-expect Granny to appear in the doorway. Even after all these years, I can feel her presence here, like a quiet warmth in the air.

As I cross the threshold, I softly whisper, "Thank you, Granny," just like I do every time I enter this charming and calming home. It's such a contrast to the life I've lived these past five years, and I welcome it. This farmhouse, which has loved me since birth, is helping me rediscover the Alex I let slip away but am now determined to reclaim.

Sinking into my leather Chesterfield sofa, I exhale deeply and think, *"What a day."* I boarded the plane in Savannah at 6 am, and now, it's 3:30 in the afternoon, and I'm finally home.

The long layover in Atlanta felt like it lasted forever. Taking the train might have been quicker.

"Oh well," I say before heading to the phone. I pick up the receiver and dial the number of a florist in Chicago that I found during my delay. The line rings. "Windy City Petals, this is Agnes."

"Hello, Agnes, my name is Alex Carrington, and I'd like to order three pink orchids to be delivered to Helena Fitzgerald at Victor Voss on Wabash Avenue, please," I say as I nervously play with the phone cord.

"Okay, we can do that for you, Miss Carrington. Just a moment while I grab a pen." After a brief pause, she asks, "Would you like a note card with the orchids?"

"Yes, please." I pause to think. "Write: 'Let me know when you've purchased that case of champagne and *tossed up your white flag*.'"

Agnes asks, "Will there be anything else?"

"No, ma'am," I say as I giggle. Then I add, "I will send the money by Western Union first thing in the morning because I want them to arrive at her office by 9 or 10 am, please."

After I order the flowers, I sit back on my Chesterfield and smile as I dream of Helena. As thoughts of her drift through my mind, I am startled by my phone ringing. I reach for the receiver and answer, "Hello."

"Hi Alex, this is Lenora. How are you, sweetie? " she asks in her polite, southern, cordial voice.

"Hello, Lenora. I'm doing great. How about you?" I ask, but my mind wonders why she is calling me.

"I'm fine, hon. We all miss you," she says with her usual politeness. Then, the phone goes silent for a moment as the dreadful feeling ascends on me, pulling my psyche back to the life I left behind.

"Lenora, I'm always glad to hear your voice, but whatever the proposition is, I'm not interested. You've always been good to me, but I want to be honest as we've always been with one another."

"And I appreciate that, Alex." She pauses for a moment and then adds, "Well, I'm going to make the offer anyway, and then you can say no again."

"Okay, Lenora," I say cordially.

"Alex, honey, I know you've stepped away for a bit, but I've got an opportunity that's too good to pass up. There's a major sales conference in Miami next week, and the clients are... well, let's just say they've got deep pockets and some very specific tastes."

Suddenly, I feel physically ill. I think of Helena's tenderness and how she held me so intimately. The stark contrast between her kindness and my previous life of pleasing clients makes me gag.

"Lenora, I'm sorry, but I have to go. This is making me emotionally sick." After I hang up, I rush to the bathroom and start heaving into the toilet. Thoughts of Helena bring me to tears as I cry uncontrollably while continuing to throw up.

The room begins spinning as I grab a washcloth and soak it in cold water. I lay down against the cold tile floor—the brand-new tile I just installed a few months ago.

Lying on the tile, I hold the cool cloth to my neck and keep crying. Lenora's call brought it all back: who I am, what I've done, and what I don't deserve. I think of how safe I felt in Helena's arms, but now I am overwhelmed and gripped with fear.

Standing up, I walk back to the Chesterfield sofa and then collapse as I continue to sob while keeping the cool cloth against my neck. It's been months since I left the high-class escort life, and I never want to return to that world.

As I lie on the sofa, I feel the comfort of my Granny in this room where we had so many heart-to-heart talks. I reach for a throw blanket, cover myself with it, and close my eyes, hoping that the sickness from Lenora's call will have faded when I wake.

It's around 7 o'clock at night. I woke up about an hour ago and immediately showered, letting the warm water cascade over my body, cleaning the context of Lenora's phone call off of me. She's always been kind to me, but it's come at a very high price.

Sitting on my front porch, I hear the rustling of the crisp fallen leaves and an occasional cricket in the distance. Sipping on a warm cup of coffee, my mind always drifts to Helena, and each time, I smile and remember her tenderness.

Walking back inside, I grab my suitcase, open it, and pull out the pouch full of the sparkling Aquamarines I sourced while I was in Savannah. The uniqueness of these gems' being from that area will add to the appeal of my high-end buyers. I need to source Gold and Silver for the bracelets and brooches I have designed and then find a manufacturer to make prototypes.

Originally, I had two manufacturers chosen: one in New York and the other in Miami. As I gaze at my beautiful gems, my business brain and heart think of Chicago. Yes, they most likely have excellent manufacturers there, as well as that sexy Helena Fitzgerald. I grin as I let the stones gently fall from my hand into the pouch.

Knowing that I will call manufacturers tomorrow in Chicago, I turn on my phonograph and put on my Glenn Miller album. The *Chattanooga Choo-Choo* begins to play, and suddenly, I feel like dancing. As I try to coordinate the East Coast swing in tempo with the song, I can't help but laugh because I can't now, nor ever could I dance. But I keep at it anyway because I'm thinking of Helena, and she makes me happy.

In the middle of one of the *Choo-Choos*, the phone rings. Still laughing, I turn off the phonograph, rush to the telephone, and answer, "Hello," I say breathlessly.

"Well, hello, Miss Carrington," Helena says with her soothing voice.

"Helena!" I shout out energetically.

"You sound out of breath; what were you doing, love?" She asks sweetly.

Immediately, I sit cross-legged on the sofa and begin twirling the phone cord as I grin. "Well, to be honest, I was dancing," I say, then laugh.

"Dancing?" Helena replies with a chuckle. Then adds, "I hate that I missed that."

Bravely, I reply, "Well, maybe you and I can dance together sometime."

"I love that idea and prefer a very slow song, Alex."

"Hmmm, I like how that sounds, Helena, and I can feel you in my arms."

We both get quiet for a moment and then Helena softly says, "I miss you., Alex." My heart immediately aches for her as I fight back the urge to cry.

I simply whisper, "I miss you too, Helena."

"Good. It makes me happy knowing you miss me," she replies sweetly. Then adds, "By the way, I enjoyed the note you left for me, and I plan on buying that case of champagne tomorrow just in case you're in the neighborhood sometime."

Pulling my legs up against me, I immediately feel anxious and go silent. "Alex, are you okay, love?" She asks sweetly.

"Yes, I'm fine. I just got a bit choked up for a minute." I pause to collect myself, then add, "I might actually be in the neighborhood."

"In Chicago?! When Alex?!" She asks excitedly.

"Perhaps soon, I had a manufacturer in New York and one in Miami that I had picked out to make my prototypes, but I thought earlier there has to be one in Chicago."

"Oh, Alex, there are several here. May I help you find one?"

"Well, sure, I would like that. I also need to source my gold and silver for the bracelets. I can do that while I'm there. I sourced my Aquamarines in Savannah, so I have those."

"Alex, I don't know what to say. Well, I do know what to say. It's been a long time since a woman made me feel the way you did last night, if ever. You're very special, Alex, and I would enjoy seeing you again soon."

"I would like that too, Helena. By the way, have you decided whether or not you are *tossing out your white flag?*" I ask with a giggle.

Helena Chuckles then gets quiet. Then she smoothly and seriously says, "I think you know the answer to that, Alex."

"Hmmm," I hum softly, then add, "Perhaps I do." I pause momentarily before asking, "When did you get home?"

"I walked into my brownstone about thirty minutes ago. How about you, Alex?"

"The layover in Atlanta took forever. My flight left at 6 this morning, and I walked into my farmhouse at 3 o'clock."

"Your farmhouse?! Helena says with heightened joy.

"Yes, I bet you didn't expect that," I laugh. Then say, "My grandparents left it to me a couple of years ago, but I've only lived here for six months. I've updated it and enjoy living here. It's a completely different lifestyle than I'm used to, but it's something that is helping to ground me again."

"Ground you? In what way, Alex?" She asks in a surprising tone. Oh god, there is that overwhelming fear of being exposed. It's just a simple question, but suddenly, my anxiety and fear freeze me, and I go silent.

"Alex, I'm sorry if I am prying, love. I don't mean to make

you uncomfortable." I know she senses something isn't right, which makes it worse.

Quickly, I pull myself back and reply, "You're not prying at all, Helena. I didn't like where my life was heading, so one day, I stopped and made a U-turn. The direction I turned brought me back to Chattanooga, to this wonderful old farmhouse I've loved forever. I would enjoy showing it to you one day."

"I would enjoy visiting you, Alex. It sounds magical there, so different from the city, which has been my life for as long as I can remember."

"Well, I'll tell you what. I will also purchase a case of champagne and have it here waiting for you when you visit me, which will be soon, I'm hoping."

"You never know; I might pull up in your front yard one day soon," she says amusingly. Then she adds, "I better let you go, Alex. Please get some sleep, love. You've had a long day."

Smiling, I say, "I plan on going to bed very soon. Thank you for calling, Helena. It's nice hearing your voice before I sleep."

"Yes, it is for me too. Goodnight, love."

"Goodnight, Helena."

CHAPTER 5

HELENA

S itting in my office, I gaze out the large window overlooking the top of Victor Voss' clothing factory on Wabash Avenue in the Garment District. It's 9:05 in the morning, and I've already spoken with two jewelry manufacturers I feel comfortable with—and hopefully, Alex will, too. Knowing she's considering changing her plans from New York and Miami to Chicago, I smile. Also, knowing she's doing this because of me makes me deeply happy.

As I look out my window, "the L" flashes by, and I hear the familiar clatter of the tracks as it rumbles past. This sound, a constant backdrop to my day, reminds me of my fast-paced life in Chicago. My thoughts drift to Alex, and I can almost picture her sitting contentedly on the farmhouse's front porch she spoke of. I laugh out loud because part of me can't quite imagine that exquisite beauty residing in a humble farmhouse outside of Chattanooga, Tennessee.

"Miss Fitzgerald?" I hear, turning to greet a young gentleman holding a stunning arrangement of orchids.

"Yes, I'm Helena Fitzgerald," I reply as I rise to meet him.

"These are for you, ma'am. Where would you like me to place them?" he asks politely.

I'm so overwhelmed I can barely speak. After a moment, I manage, "On my desk, please. Oh, wait a moment." I quickly hand him a gratuity, and he nods before leaving. Sitting back in my chair, I gently pull the small envelope from the arrangement. My heart leaps to Alex before my mind can even confirm it. As I open the note, a grin spreads across my face, and I burst into laughter. *"Tossed up your white flag,"* I say aloud, giggling as I shake my head. Without hesitation, I buzz my assistant, Celeste.

"Yes, ma'am?" Celeste asks, appearing at the door. Her eyes immediately light up. "Oh gosh, Helena! Who sent you those gorgeous orchids?"

"Just someone very dear to me," I reply with a soft smile.

Celeste steps closer, admiring the flowers. "Uh-huh. You know that pink orchids represent beauty, strength, and femininity, right?"

Looking at Celeste in disbelief, I glance back at the gorgeous orchids, feeling a sudden, deep longing to hold Alex in my arms again—so very tenderly. "No, I didn't know that Celeste, but thank you for the insight."

"You're more than welcome. Now, tell me who they're from."

"Oh no, I don't want my private life to become gossip fodder in the Victor Voss rumor mill."

"Your private life, huh? I see. Well, that tells me a lot."

"Hush, Celeste," I say sternly, then add, "Will you please take this cash and purchase a case of Moët & Chandon, Brut Impérial? Here are my car keys. Have them place it securely in the trunk."

Celeste looks at me like I've lost my mind. "This is a very odd request from you, Helena." She places a hand on her hip, gazing at me curiously before adding, "You're different,

Helena. What exactly happened to you in Savannah, Georgia?" She chuckles.

"That will be all, Celeste. And thank you."

Celeste glances back at the orchids, then at me, grinning. "Hmmm, well, I'm happy for you. You've looked lonely for way too long." She winks at me and leaves.

Shaking my head, I gaze at the beautiful orchids and think about Celeste's words: *Pink orchids represent beauty, strength, and femininity.* I can't help but smile, my heart full of affection for Alex.

I want to grab my phone and call Alex immediately, but I hesitate. No, I don't want to talk to her here at work. I enjoyed speaking with her in the privacy of my home last night. So, I decide to wait until tonight, but I know without a doubt that I want to hear her sweet voice again before I sleep.

It's eight o'clock. I've had my dinner and a glass of wine, waiting until now to call Alex. For some reason, I'm more nervous tonight—perhaps because of the orchids.

Walking to my favorite sapphire-blue velvet club chair, I sit down and pick up the telephone, waiting for the operator to connect me.

After a few moments, I hear Alex's angelic voice. "Hello?"

"I love my orchids, Alex. Thank you—they're absolutely beautiful."

"You received them? That's great, and I'm so glad you love them. Orchids are very beautiful yet strong. They remind me of you, Helena. Especially the pink ones," she says in her charming tone.

"They're lovely, Alex. It was very thoughtful of you, love."

"I wanted to make you happy and hopefully make you smile. Did they?"

"They did more than make me smile, Alex. You haven't left my thoughts all day," I whisper softly.

"Oh, Helena, that's so sweet of you. I'm happy they made you feel that way."

"They made me feel amazing, love. What did you do today?" I ask with a smile.

"Well, I fed the goats and cows, gathered all my eggs, and then milked Bessie."

"You *what*?!" I ask, completely caught off guard.

Alex bursts into laughter uncontrollably. "Oh, Helena. I wish I could have seen your face just now!" Her laughter is infectious, and I find myself chuckling.

"You got me good, Alex," I say, smiling.

"I'm sure it's funny enough to you that I live in a farmhouse in Chattanooga, Tennessee, but to think I might have all those animals would most likely make you run.

"Not necessarily, my dear," I chuckle.

"Hmmm. Oh, really?" Alex teases sweetly.

"Yes, really. You're quite a catch, Miss Carrington. It would take more than a few farm animals to scare me away."

Suddenly, the line goes silent. "Alex, are you okay?"

"Hmmm? Yes, of course," she replies, but her tone has shifted from playful to serious in an instant. What changed?

"Darling, are you sure? I feel like something's wrong," I ask, my concern growing.

Alex quickly replies, "Nothing's wrong, Helena. I'm just happy to hear from you, that's all."

"Well, I'll call you every night if it makes you happy, love."

"Oh, Helena, I could talk with you all night, but you'd go broke from the phone charges."

"Then I'll go broke because I love hearing your sweet

voice drifting softly through the night air all the way from Chattanooga to Chicago, my love."

"Helena," she whispers gently. Then, she falls silent again. I stay quiet, giving her the space to speak.

"I miss you," she whispers, and I can hear the light sound of her tears.

"Darling, please don't cry. And I miss you, my beautiful Alex."

I wait for a moment, then try to lighten the mood. "I found two potential jewelry manufacturers here in Chicago that can make your prototypes," I say in an upbeat tone.

"Oh really? That's great, Helena. Wow, that was fast!" she says excitedly.

"Well, it's for selfish reasons too," I tease.

Alex giggles. "What are the selfish reasons, Miss Fitzgerald?"

"I want to see you, Alex!" I exclaim.

"And what else?" she asks, her voice laced with a seductive undertone.

"Hmm, let me think," I say, smiling. Then, more softly, I add, "I want to hold you in my arms again, Alex. I want to gaze into your midnight eyes and thread my fingers through your raven hair. And I especially want to drink champagne with you so we can giggle together all night."

"Oh, Helena, I can't stop thinking about you," she confesses in a whisper.

"Neither can I, Alex," I reply tenderly. Then ask, "When can you come, darling?" My desire to see her swells inside me.

"I don't know. I can come anytime. I can't keep perfecting these sketches for the next month—they're ready now."

"Yes, they looked so detailed and polished when you showed them to me in Savannah. Alex, they're going to be absolutely beautiful," I say, then pause, taking a deep breath

33

before continuing. "Can you come on Friday? That way, we can spend the weekend together before you meet with the manufacturers next week."

"Yes, I can come on Friday, but I will take the train. All the layovers will be too exhausting, so I'll check the schedule and let you know when it departs."

"Oh, Alex, I can't believe you'll be here this weekend!" I say, filled with delight.

"Should I book a hotel suite?" she asks.

"Um, no, you definitely should not book a hotel room, love. I have plenty of room in my brownstone," I reply with a glint of playfulness.

Alex begins to laugh, and her infectious laughter prompts me to laugh with her. "You're simply adorable, Alex. Even back then, you were adorable to me," I say.

"You're making me blush," she replies.

"Good. Because I'm blushing too, and I'm beyond excited that you're coming this weekend."

"Helena, I will say goodnight before these calls cost you a fortune. I'll sort everything out tomorrow and call you in the evening with all the details."

"Okay, darling. That sounds perfect. I hope you sleep well."

"You too, Helena. Goodnight, sweetheart," she whispers.

"Goodnight, love," I say, gently placing the receiver back in its cradle. Reaching for my glass of Pinot Noir, I can't help but smile and let out a soft giggle. *What has that young woman done to me?* I think to myself.

As I replay the call, I hear her sweet voice again: *"Goodnight, sweetheart."* Alex just called me *sweetheart*. With that thought lingering, I head to the bathroom for a long bath to soothe my aches, but mostly to think of Alex as I'm lost in a tub full of warm suds.

CHAPTER 6

ALEX

Friday 7 am

I'm on the Chattanooga Choo Choo, which will take me to Chicago. The train left Chattanooga Union Station at 7 AM, so I should arrive around 7 or 8 PM tonight. Glancing at my watch, I see it's around noon, so I'll go to the dining car for lunch.

Seated at a dining table, I watch the trees lining the tracks with red, orange, and yellow leaves as we enter the state of Kentucky. Watching the beautiful tapestry of colors, I see a young woman around my age with soft waves of brown hair approaching me.

"Good afternoon, hon! What can I get for you today?" she asks pleasantly.

"How are you?" I ask politely.

"I'm just fine, and you? She replies.

"Oh, I'm fine, thank you." After exchanging pleasantries, I order the fried chicken and turn my gaze back out the window, letting the stunning rolling hills of Kentucky sweep past me. But soon, my thoughts drift to the captivating Helena.

Glancing at my watch again, I see I have about 7 to 8 hours until I reach Chicago. My heart races and a huge grin spreads across my face at the thought of seeing her again. Why do I feel this way? She's just a woman, and I've been with others, but this woman makes me feel both incredibly nervous and completely safe at the same time.

I can't help but chuckle; I'm giddy like a teenager. I need to pull myself together before I look like a complete fool in front of her. Well, she already knows she unnerves me, so she probably won't think much of it, hopefully.

I've thought of her so many times through the years because my crush on her didn't end when I left Victor Voss. I fantasized about that gorgeous blonde for years, and when I would pleasure myself, she was always the woman I would think of when I orgasmed. I smile at the thought of all those countless fantasies about Helena Fitzgerald, then grin.

My waitress arrives with my food. She sits down for my lunch, and I smile at her. "This looks delicious. It's been forever since I've had fried chicken," I tell her.

"Well, it's good, hon, so eat up," she says.

"Ma'am, may I leave a short note with you to be telegraphed to someone in Chicago?

"Well, sure, hon, I'll take it back in a bit. You got it ready, now?" She asks as she looks at me curiously.

"Yes, I do. I have the name and where to send it, and here are two dollars to cover the charge for the telegram and for your kindness in helping me.

She gives me a big smile and says, "Well, thank you, hon. I'll get it back there in a few minutes.

She glances at my note, which reads:

To: Helena Fitzgerald: Victor Voss on Wabash Avenue
From: A
November 12, 1949
Message:
Thoughts of you flood my mind as the train rushes to Chicago. Can't wait to be in your arms again and have my midnight eyes on you. Please have our champagne chilled!
Yours always,
A

The waitress looks at the note and then back at me. She gives me a wink and says, "Aren't you a romantic?" Leaning closer, she whispers, "She must be an extraordinary lady, 'Miss A.'" With a grin, she adds, "Don't you worry, hon. I'll make sure Miss Fitzgerald gets her telegram."

"Thank you so much," I reply with a smile before turning to my plate and digging into the fried chicken I've loved since I was a kid.

After lunch, I retreat to my private Pullman room and rest on the sofa. Outside, the beautiful landscape, farms, and pastureland slip by as the train glides along the tracks. I close my eyes, and there she is—Helena. I can almost feel her tender lips against mine as the soothing rumble of the train's wheelsets echoes beneath me.

The rhythmic clickety-clack lulls me into a dreamy haze, and I imagine Helena holding me close, my head resting against her. The taste of rich champagne lingers on my lips, and the scent of her Chanel perfume mingled with her unique aroma, fills the air as I rest against the cool window, eyes closed.

Drifting off yet acutely aware of the miles still separating Helena and me, I find myself reminiscing about young Alex

—so pure and brimming with dreams. I don't reach back for her often because I know I've let her down. I haven't fulfilled the many wonderful dreams she had for me. The plans she envisioned have been marred by greed and the desperate need to meet others' beauty standards. How foolish I've been.

As a tear drips, I remember how it all went wrong, so I open my eyes quickly and divert my attention to the picturesque views of the countryside. As the train crosses the Illinois River, I gaze into the brown, murky water and see my reflection. *That's the color of your soul now, brown and muddy; my* mind churns at me again.

Forcing my mind to Helena's beautiful face, I see her smiling at me, unaware of my turmoil within. She doesn't see me like this but doesn't know the truth. *It's been six months; do I really have to reveal my past to her?* I think to myself.

Suddenly, a wave of nausea hits me, prompting me to stand and pace in my small compartment. I try to focus on Granny and the happiness at my farmhouse—my refuge, where I've always felt loved unconditionally. As I pace, I realize I must accept who I am now and make peace with the past. I need to apologize to young Alex for straying so far off course.

Sitting back on the sofa, I close my eyes and picture young Alex—about sixteen, lounging in her bedroom, lost in the sounds of Billie Holiday and others wafting from the radio, just as she does every night. I sit beside her on the bed, and she turns to me with a smile, asking, "Hi, who are you?"

Grinning back, I thread my fingers gently through her hair and reply, "Someone who loves you and wants to apologize for letting you down."

Young Alex studies me, her expression curious yet understanding. She takes my hand, beams, and says, "Now I know who you are. Don't worry; you simply got off course for a while. There's no need to apologize. I'm proud that you've found your way back to me." I lean down and kiss her head sweetly, then open my eyes.

Laughter and tears mingle as I feel an immense burden lifting from my soul. I feel free and light, the past behind me. The future is where I'm headed, and with *The Alex Collection* and Helena Fitzgerald, that future is very bright. I see it clearly.

~

As we approach Union Station, meeting Helena is making me somewhat nervous. Even though we have spent the last several nights speaking on the telephone about how much we miss one another, I still feel unnerved. I know Helena says she misses me, and I remember what she said on the first telephone call. *It's been a very long time since a woman made me feel the way you did last night, if ever.*

I grin at that thought as the train comes to a stop, my heart racing with anticipation. Gathering myself, I stand and disembark. The moment I step onto the platform, my eyes lock onto Helena—my beautiful blonde, my older woman— the one I realize at this very moment that I've loved since I was 25, smiling at me with her sparkling steel-blue eyes. Her soft, blonde hair falls gracefully, perfectly framed by a chic, black knee-length overcoat cinched at the waist, accentuating her shapely, feminine figure. She takes my breath away.

Helena opens her arms, and I walk swiftly into them. Stirring by the day's anxious anticipation, my emotions build to a crescendo. As she holds me close, I feel overwhelmed, the flood of everything hitting me at once. I try to steady myself, but she gently pulls back, her eyes searching mine as she whispers, "Alex, my love, are you alright?"

"Yes, it's just been a long day, and I'm so happy to see you, Helena," I say as I try not to weep. Helena pulls me close,

39

holding me tight, obviously aware of her effect on me and how she calms me because she isn't releasing me.

She whispers, "Alex, I'm so happy you're here. I've thought of nothing but you all day—all week."

"Oh, Helena, I feel foolish," I confess to her. Then add, "It's just been a long train ride."

"Well, you should never feel that way with me, Alex. You're a beautiful and wonderful woman, and I'm crazy about you," she says softly. Pulling away gently, she gazes into my eyes and adds, "And I'm taking you home with me right now. Come on, let's get your luggage."

After we secure my luggage from baggage claim, a porter helps us load it into the trunk of Helena's Cadillac. Once inside the car, my gaze is fixed on her, and she keeps glancing at me, smiling, then sweetly says, "I'm so glad you're here, Alex, and I received that sweet telegram around 4 o'clock today. You're such a romantic. It made me smile, love, but I must confess it also moved me sensually."

"Good, because that was my plan," I say playfully, giving Helena a wink. Glancing around and noticing no one nearby, I lean in and gently pull her toward me, pressing my lips to hers in a tender kiss.

With a grin, she says, "Like I told you a minute ago, Alex, I'm taking you home with me right now, love!" She exclaims as she puts the car in drive.

With a smile, I lean toward Helena, looping my arm through hers. I maintain a grin the whole drive to her brownstone in Lincoln Park. "I've missed you, Helena," I whisper quietly.

Helena reaches for my hand, intertwines her fingers through mine, and kisses it. "I've ached for you, Alex," she says seriously. I glance at her, and our smiles turn sensual. I feel her desire for me, and I know she sees mine.

Bringing her hand to my face, I kiss it with my eyes

closed. In a soft voice, I say, "I've ached for you, Helena. Every phone call we shared left me wanting you desperately." She gives me a look I've never seen before, which stirs me in ways I can't ignore. I clasp both hands around hers, holding it tightly.

After we park in Helena's private garage, we silently walk to her brownstone. The intimate confessions we shared during the drive have rendered small talk irrelevant. We remain quiet until we step into her entryway, a spacious room with soaring ceilings.

As I set my luggage down, our eyes lock once more, and the intensity between us becomes overwhelming. "Let me take your coat, love," she says softly. I allow her to help me with my coat, and she hangs it up before quickly taking hers off.

"You look amazing, Helena, but then again, you always do," I say with a smile.

She smiles at me, takes my hand, and says, "Come on, you. Let's have that champagne. It's been chilling since last night."

She stops us just before we reach the kitchen, pulls me close, and kisses me sweetly. Then she softly says, "When you disembarked the train, you completely took my breath away, Alex. I've thought of nothing else but you all week, my love."

CHAPTER 7

HELENA

Holding Alex's hand, we walk into the sitting room. "Please have a seat, Alex," I say as I sit on the sofa. Opening the champagne, I grin and add, "I simply can't believe you are here in my home, Alex."

She smiles sweetly and replies, "Neither can I, Helena. I've been somewhat nervous all day on the train ride, I must admit."

Handing her a flute of champagne, I move closer to her, rest my arm on the back of the sofa, and gaze at her. "I've been nervous too, Alex. I must admit."

Alex gives me a light chuckle. "You have? I mean, Helena, you're always composed and calm. Why were you nervous?"

Threading her fingers through my hair, she whispers, "You, Alex. You're obviously unaware of what you do to me, love."

With her bright laugh, she shakes her head and replies, "I suppose so, but I'm glad I have that effect on you."

"I think it's your turn to make our toast, Alex," I say as I continue feeling her soft loose curls of raven hair through my fingers.

"Well, okay, let me think." As I gaze at her, I can't help but want to take her to my bed and love her. I can't even imagine how beautiful and amazing making love with her will be.

Alex touches my flute with hers, then softly says, "Let's toast to new beginnings." Touched by her words, I gently kiss her cheek, inhaling her scent. It's Caron Pour Un Homme, but her body's unique warmth adds a richer, muskier depth that blends beautifully with the bergamot and lavender.

Holding my flute against hers with our eyes locked, I whisper, "To new beginnings, love." With eyes still locked, we sip our champagne.

Alex nestles back against the sofa and grins. "This takes me back to Savannah, Helena. Do you want to get me tipsy again?"

Laughing, I say, "Yes, I must admit that I do, but I'll be tipsy as well, so don't worry." Alex laughs at me

Leaning into Alex, I smell her aroma again. "My god, you smell delicious, Alex, but may I ask you something?"

"Of course."

"Well, let me rephrase that. Alex, you are the only woman I've ever known who wears a man's fragrance. I noticed it right away. You're wearing Caron Pour Un Homme, aren't you?"

Alex chuckles, "I guess you caught me. Only you would be able to detect that, Helena. And yes, I am indeed wearing that cologne."

"Well, it smells amazing on you, Alex. However, I would love to know why you prefer wearing a male fragrance."

As she grins at me, Alex takes our flutes of champagne and sets them on the coffee table. She moves closer to me and humorously says, "Because I want to be your man, Helena Fitzgerald."

We roar with laughter, lightening the mood, "Oh dear lord, Alex, that's hilarious."

"Well, I already have a man's name and wear men's cologne, so see, I'm halfway there," she says with laughter.

I shake my head and say, "Alex, you're hysterical." Continuing our laughter, Alex wraps her arms around my neck and moves closer.

"No, I simply don't like how women's fragrances smell on me. I never have. It must be my body chemistry; it seems to merge better with masculine scents. Do you like the fragrance on me?" She asks.

Pulling her to me, I whisper, "Alex, your aroma intoxicates me, so yes. I absolutely love it on you, baby."

"Good," she softly whispers against my cheek. With Alex's arms around my neck, I reach around her body and pull her against me. Our lips meet again. There are those sweet lips I remember from Savannah, the ones that taste of champagne and sweet nectar, unmistakably her own flavor.

As I pull her into me, our lips open, and I feel her soft, warm tongue brush against mine. My soul is burning with pain that pulses through me, looking for an escape. Finding nowhere to run, the sensual pain settles firmly against my feminine soul into one erotic mass of pleasure.

My fingers want to touch every strand of Alex's raven hair. Threading through her curls, I kiss her deeply as she pushes her body against mine. Alex breaks our kiss and gazes into my eyes with an almost haunting seriousness.

I whisper, "Alex, baby, are you okay?"

She nods, kisses my cheek, and then slowly pulls away. Pulling her back to me, I softly say, "Alex, I know you've had a long day, and we are both tired. Baby, I am not expecting anything more than this tonight."

"Helena," she whispers. Gazing at me, she adds, "I am tired. I agree, but I must admit it's taking a lot of restraint to wait. However, you're right. Let's just drink our champagne tonight and enjoy one another as we are doing now."

I wink at her, smile, and whisper, "Yes, my love. That sounds wonderful."

"Helena?"

"Yes, love?" I ask softly.

Alex picks up our champagne flutes, hands me mine, and then touches her flute against mine. She gazes at me and whispers, "Helena, when we make love, I have no doubt it will be the most beautiful moment I've ever experienced."

Hypnotized by her midnight eyes and the words she just whispered to me, I'm immediately gripped by Alex's allure, and I completely freeze. Never has any other woman moved me like this or gripped me with such complete submission.

"Are you alright, Helena?" She asks sweetly. All I can do is nod and then take two sips of champagne to help calm me. As I sip the champagne, I think, *"How in the hell could I even perform tonight anyway?"* This woman has me completely spellbound.

Trying to break her spell over me, I quickly ask, "Alex, are you hungry?"

"No, I ate a small meal on the train at about 5 o'clock, but If you're hungry, let's get you something to eat."

"I'm fine. I had a snack about 6 this evening, so I'm not hungry," I say as I take another sip of champagne and begin to feel more like myself again.

Alex and I continue talking, finishing our bottle of champagne, as we share many intimate kisses over the next couple of hours, enjoying just being together. Glancing at my watch, I say, "It's 10:30. Are you sleepy, Alex?"

"Yes, but not enough to give you up for the evening," She says sweetly as she touches my cheek and smiles at me.

Threading my fingers again through her dark hair, I gaze into those midnight gems and say, "Well, we are both committed to waiting to make love, correct?"

Alex looks at me, somewhat puzzled, but says, "Yes, we are. Why do you ask?'

Moving to the edge of the couch to give Alex some space, I take a deep breath and say, "Well, I was thinking we could take another chilled bottle of champagne upstairs."

Alex grins and slowly says, "Okay." She gazes into my eyes, knowing my desires. She whispers, "Yes, I'd love to drink champagne and sleep beside you, Helena."

As I exhale loudly. Alex laughs her delightful bright laugh, and I say, "Thank you for making that so much easier for me, Alex."

Alex pulls me against her and holds me tightly. "I'm so crazy about you, Helena. I've spent days away from you since Savannah. All I want is to be right beside you." Leaning into Alex, I pull her face to me and give her an intense kiss—a kiss so deep that our souls touch. Our hearts are so close they can speak to one another.

Pulling away, Alex's eyes meet mine, and she whispers, "My god, Helena, perhaps I should sleep in the spare bedroom." Then she bursts into laughter.

Standing, I reach for her hand and say, "No, ma'am, you've already committed to sharing my bed with me, Miss Carrington. Alex stands and chuckles.

With a charming grin, she says, "You grab the champagne, Helena, and I'll get my suitcase. Okay?" I give her a nod and head to the kitchen with a wide smile.

With my pajamas as I sit on the side of the bed, I glance up and see Alex coming from the en suite. "Hi, love. More champagne?"

As she approaches me, she smiles at me, and I gaze up at her, handing her a flute of champagne. "You're so beautiful, Helena," she says sweetly, then leans down and kisses my cheek. I giggle at her as she kneels before me.

Alex rests her arms against my legs, looks up at me,

smiles, and asks, "Is this wise sharing a bed with champagne, Helena?" Then she gives me that bright laugh.

"No. Probably not, but we've made a pact," I reply as I lean down and smell her raven hair. "Come on, love, crawl in beside me," I add.

Alex and I turn on our sides with champagne in hand and gaze at one another. "It's hard to drink champagne lying down, Helena."

Laughing, I say, "Let's try." As we both try drinking sideways from the glass, we get completely tickled and spill champagne on the bed sheets. Alex bursts into laughter, sits her flute on her side table, and falls on her back, laughing uncontrollably.

"Damn!" I say, "All over my clean sheets!" Alex roars with laughter. "Let me get a towel," I add with a displeased, frantic tone.

Alex continues laughing as I try to dry the sheets, "Why are you continuing to laugh? I know it's more than wet sheets," I chuckle.

Alex rises and helps me with the sheets. She continues laughing and says, "Because you sound like Helena from years ago." Then she falls back against the bed and roars again.

"I do, huh?

Alex grabs me and says, "Yes! Just like the old Helena—the one with her strict and demanding tone. The one I fell in love with years ago," she confesses, her laughter easing as our eyes lock.

"Alex, my love," I say softly but surprisingly.

Alex sits on the edge of the bed and quickly says, "I'm sorry, Helena. I shouldn't have said that." I immediately rush to her, get on my knees in front of her, and grasp her hands.

"Why shouldn't you have said that, Alex? I ask softly.

As I gaze at her, our eyes lock. "It just came out, but I

won't take it back because I did fall in love with you years ago, and I'm still in love with you even more now, Helena."

Sitting beside her, I see her eyes glistening. I touch her cheek, turn her face toward me, and smile at this lovely woman. Looking into her deep midnight eyes, I feel the love I have for her, and I softly say, "Alex, I am deeply in love with you. I fell for you the minute you approached me in the hotel lobby in Savannah, my love."

"You're in love with me, Helena?"

Nodding, I lean in and kiss her tenderly, tasting the champagne on her soft lips. "Yes, I'm in love with you, Alex, and now I understand why I missed you so much when you left Victor Voss seven years ago."

"Helena," she whispers softly, then turns her head. "Helena Fitzgerald's in love with me," she quietly murmurs to herself, her voice filled with surprise.

Kneeling in front of her again, I gaze up into those dark eyes and softly say, "Of course, I'm in love with you, Alex. How could I not be? You're everything I've ever wanted in a woman. And I've waited so long for you."

CHAPTER 8

ALEX

Gazing down at Helena, I try to process her words, but my mind struggles. Yet, as I look into her steel-blue eyes, I realize that my heart has heard every syllable of her proclamation of love for me. "Helena," I whisper as I smile at her.

Slipping off the bed, I grab her around her neck and begin to laugh as her arms encircle my waist, pulling me firmly against her with incredible strength.

"I love you, Alex Carrington," she whispers against my ear. As I grin, I hug her with equal force, feeling her womanly body against mine. I inhale her sensual aroma, which captivates me and stirs me sensually. Pulling away to gaze at her, I see her desire for me, but I know I can't give in, so I pull her in and hug her again.

Overcome by her love for me and my ugly past, I begin to cry, and I can't stop myself no matter how hard I try.

"Alex, my love. Darling, what's wrong?" She asks delicately. I simply hold her, unwilling to allow her to look at me.

Helena pulls away almost forcefully, looks at me, and says, "Alex, you must tell me what is bothering you, my love."

"I can't," I faintly whisper, then collapse against her. Helena pulls my body to her, threading her fingers through my hair, and gently rubs my back to soothe me. She remains quiet for a while, allowing me to sob. Occasionally saying, "Alex, my love."

As she consoles me. My sobbing continues. Helena softly says, "Alex, let me hold you in bed. Come on, let's get up."

Pulling away, she stands and reaches for my hand. Taking her hand, I gaze up at her and see her genuine love and care for me, and I realize this is the moment. With tears in my eyes and my heart laid bare, I remain on the cool wood floor and confess, "Helena, up until six months ago, I was an escort, a high-class call girl, and had been for five years." Then I pull my hand away and curl into a cocoon, crying in despair, knowing I've just lost the woman I've loved forever.

Suddenly, I feel Helena wrap her warm body and arms around me from behind, and I hear her whisper softly, "I know, Alex."

She knows I think to myself as I continue crying. Helena holds me tightly, my body depleted from tears, despair, and shame. She simply continues to love me. Finally, I offer a faint, "How did you know, Helena? And why would you still love me?"

Helena pulls me up, and we both stand, but I can't bring myself to gaze at her. "Alex, please look at me."

As I meet her gaze, I search her face and eyes for signs of disgust, but all I see is the same Helena I've always known, even after confessing my ugly truth. "How could you know this, Helena?" I ask in disbelief.

Taking my hand, she says, "Come on, Alex, let's drink our champagne." As she fills our flutes, I grab some tissue and begin to dry my face and eyes. "Come here, baby," she says, touching the bed and inviting me to sit beside her.

Sitting beside her, I taste the champagne, and it brings back memories of Savannah—our first time in her room, drinking our first glass together. Helena sets her flute on the bedside table, then wraps her arms around my waist and pulls me close. She holds me tenderly and softly says, "I don't know how I knew, Alex. There were times when you went silent during our telephone calls. Perhaps it was because you didn't want to be intimate with me that night in Savannah. And there were countless clues in statements that you made."

Remaining silent, Helena continues, "One day, it dawned on me that it was possible. At first, I struggled with the *'what ifs'* if it were true. Then I realized it didn't matter because I knew it was part of your past. More importantly, I realized that I was in love with you. I also knew you would tell me before we became intimate because I felt your love for me. That realization made me love you even more, Alex. And I was right."

Nodding as she holds me, I ask faintly, "Where do we go from here, Helena?

"Right where we are, Alex. I just professed my love for you, darling, and I meant every word of it. I am deeply in love with you, Alex Carrington, and nothing could ever tarnish my pure love for you."

The following day, I awake to the soft light dancing on the ceiling, streaming through the slightly open shutters. Thoughts of my confession to Helena flood back, weighing heavily on my heart and mind. Helena held me close all night, loving me as I slept. Each time I stirred, I felt encased in her arms, her grip strong and confident.

The rich aroma of coffee and food fills the air as I rise and open my suitcase. Slipping on my gray silk robe, I retrieve a black velvet pouch, tuck it into the pocket of my robe, and head downstairs to find Helena. Though shame lingers, the love she offered me last night and her commitment to loving me make it bearable.

"Good morning, love," she says as I enter the kitchen. I walk into her arms, craving the nurturing only she can provide. Without hesitation, she whispers, "I love you, Alex."

"Breakfast smells delicious, and so do you," I reply as I kiss her cheek.

Grinning, she asks, "Would you like coffee?"

"Yes, but I'll get it." Helena nods and smiles at me as she continues preparing our breakfast. I pour her more coffee, fill my cup, and then lean against the counter, gazing at her. "You look beautiful this morning," I say with a grin.

"Thank you, darling. So do you," she says, her gaze constant and loving. Then she adds, "You make me so happy, Alex."

Feeling a bit bashful, I simply grin and look into my coffee, but I feel the tears. I know Helena is being exceptionally tender with me this morning because of last night. Sitting my cup on the counter, I approach her from behind, encircle her, and inhale her scent. "I smelled you all night, Helena," I whisper, then I add, "More importantly, I felt you. I don't believe you let go of me once. Each time I woke, I felt safe, engulfed in your love."

Helena turns the gas eye off, pushes the skillet of food back, and then turns toward me. She grabs me, pulls me against her, and forcefully kisses me with a force so strong that I'm unsure it's even her. Locking my arms around her waist, I grip and squeeze her with every ounce of my strength. Our kiss ignites; our desire is raw and untamed.

Helena's early morning passion for me is the only nourishment I need, so I greedily feed on her.

She threads her fingers through my hair as she continues pushing her warm tongue against mine. My tongue dances with hers as I lower my hands to her ass and firmly grasp it as I pull her against my feminine essence. My head protests somewhat, but my heart and the pulsating in my sexual region are under her complete domination.

Helena breaks our kiss, and I moan into her soft blonde hair, breathlessly whispering, "Helena, I've wanted you for so long, baby."

She grabs two small plates and quickly fills them with food, then says, "Grab your coffee and that juice, and follow me, love."

Within minutes, we're back in her warm bed, indulging in our breakfast while giggling. After only a few bites, I gather our plates and set them on my nightstand, then pour each of us a glass of juice as I grin.

Helena leans toward me, her voice low and seductive. "Will that give you enough nourishment for the day, love?" Her lips brush against mine as she whispers, "You might need more food, Alex. You obviously have no idea how much I crave you."

"Then I'll be forced to devour you," I say playfully.

Helena laughs and then asks, "What's sticking out of the pocket of your robe, Miss Carrington?" I glance down and see the velvet pouch hanging halfway out.

Grinning, I meet her steel-blue gaze, which are filled with a potent mix of desire and curiosity. I must decide quickly: do I break this heated moment to give her my gift, or wait until later? My romantic heart pulls me toward the velvet pouch, and I smile at her. "It's a very special gift for you, Helena."

She grins. "You spoil me, Alex. Flowers, letters, telegrams, and now this."

"You should be spoiled, Miss Fitzgerald. A woman like you deserves it every day of her life," I say with conviction, placing the velvet pouch into her hands.

With a grin, she asks, "What is it, Alex?"

"The first of *The Alex Collection*, sweetheart," I reply, brushing my thumb gently against her cheek.

Helena pulls out a gold chain with a sparkling aquamarine pendant and gasps, "Alex!"

Gazing into her eyes, I gently say, "My collection will be bracelets, but you will have this one-of-a-kind gold necklace with my signature aquamarine pendant, sweetheart.""Alex, I don't know what to say. This is the most beautiful necklace I've ever seen. When—when did you have it made for me?" she asks, astonishment written all over her face. "You had this made especially for me, Alex?"

Touching her face and nodding, I say, "I'm so in love with you, Helena. How could I not give you the first piece made by *The Alex Collection*? Here, let me put it around your neck." Facing her, I reach around, our faces inches apart as I clasp the necklace.

"Have you noticed the color of the aquamarine stone, Helena?"

"Of course, Alex. They're beautiful gems; they remind me of the ocean," she says, looking down at the pendant.

Holding the pendant gently, I gaze into her eyes and softly reply, "Yes, they are reminiscent of the sea, but mostly, they remind me of your eyes, Helena. They always have."

"Alex," she whispers faintly. Glancing at the pendant, she asks, "That can't possibly be why you chose aquamarines as your signature stone, can it?"

"Why not?" I ask, keeping my gaze locked on hers.

Helena remains silent for a moment, nodding as a single

tear drips onto the pendant. Gathering her composure, she meets my gaze and says, "Because that would mean you truly have loved me all these years, just as you've claimed." She glances back at the pendant before returning her eyes to mine and asks, "My god, Alex, why do you love me like this?"

"Well, I could sit here all day and tell you the millions of reasons why," I say smoothly as I crawl onto her, gently pressing her down against the bed with my body. Lying atop her, my eyes lock on hers as I continue, "Or I could show you the millions of reasons why right now." You choose, Miss Fitzgerald," I whisper against her lips.

Helena giggles softly, a spark of mischief in her eyes. She wraps her arms around my neck and whispers, "I'd much prefer that you show me, darling."

CHAPTER 9

HELENA

With my arms around Alex, I gaze into her midnight eyes, threading my fingers through her soft raven hair, gently pulling her toward my lips. She kisses me tenderly, slipping one arm beneath my body; she pulls me tightly into her. Our kisses remain soft and intimate.

Alex pulls back, her eyes locking onto mine as she smiles sweetly, saying, "I love you, Helena."

I touch her lips with my fingertips and whisper, "I love you, baby." I pause for a moment, seeing the vulnerability in her eyes, then gently add, "You're safe with me, Alex. You always will be, my love." Her gaze remains fixed on mine before she gives a soft, understanding nod.

Alex lowers her lips to my neck, kissing it fervently; my body responds with a deep, erotic, pleasurable ache I haven't felt in years. I grip her hair, holding her close as I moan and softly whisper, "Oh, Alex, you feel amazing."

She continues her loving caresses, playfully biting at my neck before lifting her gaze back to mine with a smile. As I focus on her lips, I tenderly brush my fingers across her lips. Alex closes her eyes, moaning softly.

Slipping off of me, Alex unties the sash of my robe. As we sit up, she removes it, and I begin untying her robe. We both giggle as we quickly undress one another, tossing our bedding attire to the end of the bed.

As I look at my young lover's body, I whisper softly, "Alex, you're beautiful."

"And you are even more gorgeous than I could have imagined, Helena. Your sexy, mature body takes my breath away." She says, then brushes her thumb across each nipple, watching them peak. She then lifts her eyes to mine and grins."

Completely nude, we lie on our sides, pulling one another close, eyes locked. I reach around Alex and pull her closer to me. Her hand finds my ass, and she begins rubbing it slowly. "You have a nice ass, Miss Fitzgerald," she says playfully.

I softly chuckle, "And you, Miss Carrington, have a very nice everything. Your breasts are incredible, Alex." As I lower my eyes to her bosoms, I add, "Dear lord, they're beautiful, love."

"Thank you, sweetheart," she says softly, and then our lips meet again. The passion increases, our lips part, and our tongues embrace as they're reunited. Moaning, I kiss Alex deeper, and she meets my loving force as she moves back on top of me.

Alex reaches for my breasts and slides her thumb across my already peaked nipples. Moaning into her mouth, I hold her tightly as the intensity of our kisses increases. Feeling her hand sliding slowly down my body, the ache in my feminine nexus begins to grow and expand. The ache is deep and begs to be loved; I breathlessly say, "Touch me, Alex. Please, baby."

As her tongue pushes against mine, I part my legs, and her hand caresses my thighs, and then her fingers find my ache. Alex immediately moves her fingers to my core finding my wetness. She slowly pulls the liquid to my clit and then moves across it delicately. Alex reaches for more liquid and repeats her movements again and again.

Making back and forth, movements against my clit, she loves me tenderly. Then she breaks our kiss to gaze and watch me. "Alex," Is all I can whisper.

"Yes, sweetheart?" She asks seductively as she keeps her fingers moving across my swollen clit. Alex rises above me; I glance at her breasts, so full and waiting to be loved. Lifting my eyes back to meet hers, she returns to my core and enters me slowly. I part my legs, Inviting her to enter me deeply.

Reaching for her breasts, I hold them firmly as Alex pushes deep inside me, and then she gazes at me, keeping her fingers still. Looking up at her, I touch her face and whisper, "I love you." She winks slowly at me but doesn't speak. With her fingers deep inside me, Alex moves to my breasts and then takes one of my nipples in her mouth.

Sucking tenderly, she begins to move inside me as her eyes find mine again. I nod and softly say, "Yes, Alex. That feels so good." Alex closes her eyes and begins sucking my nipples firmly, pushing deeply into my core. Her body, mouth, arm, and fingers become one as she starts fucking me slowly.

With my fingers entangled in her raven hair, I gaze at her and watch her love me. My entire body responds to Alex with submissive yearning and an erotic aching that increases with each thrust she lovingly inflicts deep inside me. "Yes, Alex," Is all I can say.

Pulling gently out of me, both hands cup my bosoms, and Alex sucks and loves each one with loving force. She gazes up at me as her tongue teases my nipples. All I can do is smile. Moving downward, she kisses my stomach, her fingers holding my nipples. Sitting up, I pull her to me and kiss her forcefully, my fingers still in her hair. I grab several locks and grip them tightly. Alex moans into my mouth; the vibrations of her moans give my body erotic goosebumps.

Alex breaks our kiss gently, and then she moves her back against the headboard. Grinning, I move to her then straddle her, slowly easing my body onto her. "Yes, Helena," she says with a grin. Then adds, "I've dreamt of this a million times."

Gazing at her, I see how young she is, but my thoughts quickly fade as Alex finds my sacred center, gently gathers my wetness, and then enters me even deeper than before as she gazes into my eyes.

Closing my eyes, I relax and submit to my young lover and fall against her. Alex begins gently thrusting into me as she touches my back, rubbing it soothingly. My desire deepens with each thrust. Pulling back, I look at her grasping the headboard firmly, then breathlessly whisper, "Yes, Alex. You're incredible, my young lover."

Alex immediately grabs me forcefully, and her thrusts become harder and deeper. She moves her head to my breast and places her mouth over one of my nipples, and begins sucking it as she loves me. Gripping the headboard, I watch her as my body constricts with aching erotic desire. The thrusts Alex gives me are strong and forceful. Letting go of the headboard, I put my arms around her neck. She lifts her eyes to mine, continuing to please me physically and emotionally.

"Yes, baby," I whisper as her thrust grows faster and fiercer. Alex's expression is serious and determined. "I'm close, Alex, but I want you on my clit, sweetheart."

She gently pulls out and touches my clit firmly as she moves in circles. Winking at me, she asks softly, "Like this, baby?"

"Yes, darling. I'm so close, and you're so loving with me, Alex," I say, then close my eyes and enjoy her loving me.

Feeling my orgasm peaking, I open my eyes, smile at her, and see her love. "How long have you loved me like this, Alex?" I ask tenderly.

"Since I met you, Helena," she whispers breathlessly as I feel myself falling.

"Yes, baby, come for me, sweetheart."

"I'm coming, Alex," I whisper. Touching Alex's face, I gaze into her soul and tumble straight into it. My orgasm is hard yet lovingly tender. "Alex—my sweet Alex," I say as I continue to orgasm. As It ends, I relax and fall against her, and she pulls me against her warm body. Alex holds me tightly with her strong arms wrapped completely around me.

After a moment, Alex slides down, pulling me with her. We are once again face-to-face, and she rises above me. She moves her arm underneath my neck to hold me close and then moves her fingers back to my wetness. She gathers my liquid and begins loving my clit again. I feel my body restricting with an aching warmth. She asks sweetly, "Will you come again for me, Helena?"

Before I can answer, I'm climaxing simply from hearing her voice, "Yes, Alex," I say with a moan as I come even harder than before. Grasping her face, I gaze into her eyes and say, "Fuck me, Alex." Then I turn away from her and get on my knees, fully submitting to the woman whose love I never want to know a day without.

"Yes, sweetheart, I'll fuck you," she says as she enters me from behind. As I grasp the headboard, Alex begins thrusting forcefully inside me. She grips my shoulder and starts fucking me without restraint. "Helena, you're so beautiful; I love fucking you," she asserts with a dominant voice.

Something about Alex's voice sends erotic chills over me and brings me to another unyielding orgasm as I let out a gasping moan. Lost in trying to regain some strength, Alex moved beneath me. Opening my eyes, I see her mouth at my clit. All I can do is smile. "Alex, my god. You're incredible."

Moving onto her mouth, I feel her warm tongue tenderly moving against my clit. Gazing down at her, our eyes lock, I know she wants to watch my reactions to her touch. She reaches for my hands, and our fingers intertwine.

As I move against her and feel myself peaking, I think to myself, *no one has ever made love to me like this.* Alex's tongue on my clit feels incredible; she moves it with such fluid movements. It glides smoothly back and forth across my clit with the exact amount of pressure needed to bring me to another climax.

Grasping her hands tightly, we move together in a slow dance, bringing me to another peak. "Alex—Alex, I'm coming, love," I say, then feel the release from the orgasm rush through me like a warm wave crashing inside me. All I can do is whimper and moan. Alex grabs my weak body, holding me until my orgasm is complete.

Moving from beneath me, she pulls me tenderly to the bed and spoons me against her warmth. Pulling the covers over us, she holds me tightly kissing my back and shoulders. Lying in Alex's arms, I realize what I've found with her.

Turning to face her, I thread my fingers through her hair and smile at my young love. With my fingers in her soft raven hair, I move on top of her and kiss her, holding nothing back. Pushing my tongue with passion against hers, she meets my intensity, threading her fingers through my hair. She grips my hair and breaks our kiss, pulling me away.

With eyes locked, we remain silent as our souls touch. Then I whisper, "I'm a fool; I could have had this for the past seven years."

Alex laughs softly and says, "Yes, but wasn't it worth the wait?"

Nodding, I softly reply, "Very much so, Alex."

CHAPTER 10

ALEX

"I 've wanted to love you like this forever, Helena. There's always been something about you that stirred me, something I've never been able to move beyond," I murmur as we lie wrapped in each other's arms.

Helena smiles into my eyes and softly replies, "I'm a fortunate woman, Alex. You're incredible; you could have anyone on this planet you reached for. I'll never fully understand why you chose me, but I'll always be thankful for you—that much I know."

"Well, I know why I chose you, Helena Fitzgerald, so that's all that matters."

"Alex, no one has ever made love to me the way you just loved me. I felt your passion, and desire for me, as well as your love. And my orgasms were unbelievable," I say with a huge grin.

"From the look on your face, I think I made you happy and you taste incredible, sweetheart. Making love to you was truly beautiful for me, Helena," I say. Gazing into her lovely steel-blue eyes, I add, "Thank you for holding me all night long. Your love was the medicine that I obviously needed."

Helena pulls me close, rises above me, and softly says, "Now it's my turn to show you the millions of reasons why I love you, Alex."

With a grin, I reply, "It is, huh?"

"Yes, indeed, Miss Carrington. And I'm going to devour this youthful body of yours."

"Ummm, I love how that sounds from you, but you make me a bit nervous, too," I reply as I thread my fingers through her soft blonde hair and gaze at her steel-blue eyes.

Helena looks at me and asks sweetly, "Why, Alex? It's me, baby, and I'm completely and hopelessly in love with you."

"Because I've been in love with you for so long, Helena," I say a bit nervously. Then add, "Sometimes, I still feel like that 25-year-old who is completely lovestruck by you."

"Alex," she whispers lovingly.

Holding her hand and glancing away, I ask, "Does that sound silly?" When I look back at Helena, she is nodding and smiling at me. She touches my lips, delicately tracing their outline.

Helena moves on top of me, wrapping her arms around me as she whispers, "Put your arms around me, Alex, and hold me tightly." I do as she asks. Then, Helena begins kissing my cheek before moving to my ear and whispering, "I love you, Alex. Take some deep breaths and relax for me, love. We have all day, baby."

As I breathe deeply, Helena rises and looks into my eyes, smiling. Seeing the love in her gaze, I pull her to my lips, opening them to feel her warm love and soft tongue caressing mine. Helena moves her hand to my breasts and cups one of them tenderly as she continues kissing me deeply.

Moaning into her mouth, I feel her desire for me increase as well as my own. Every muscle in me constricts with erotic aching for this woman. My feminine soul pulses and aches, wanting to be touched and loved by this woman. Pulling away to gaze at me, Helena asks softly, "Are you okay, Alex?"

Touching her face, I reply, "Yes, as I said before, you're obviously the medicine I need." While smiling at me, Helena nods and then gently moves her hand down my body, caressing it. She caresses my bosoms, my stomach, and down to my thighs. Helena loves me with her mature strength, which I crave.

"You feel incredible, Alex. Everything is so beautiful with you, my love," she says tenderly. "Will you lie on your stomach for me?"

Giggling as I turn over, I say, "Helena, I'd probably do almost anything you ask of me, sweetheart." She laughs and begins massaging my back and ass as she lies beside me.

"My God, you're a damn knockout, Alex. Loving you like this is unbelievable," Helena says," as she softly chuckles.

"Why did you laugh?" I ask, giggling.

"Alex, it's as if you slipped from the heavens, and I just happened to be the fortunate one to catch you as you tumbled. How I ever won your love is a mystery," she replies seriously.

Turning my head to gaze at Helena, I whisper, "I believe that's the kindest thing anyone has ever said to me, sweetheart."

"I meant every word of it, Alex."

Smiling at her I relax and enjoy Helena's love. After she massages me for a while, I turn back and face her. She immediately pulls me to her and kisses me fervently. With one hand is in my hair, the other travels to my sacred gateway. Opening my legs for her, she enters and finds my overabundance of wetness that gathered during her orgasms.

She whispers on my lips, "You're soaked, love. How did that happen?" She seductively teases me.

"I don't have a clue, sweetheart," I whisper, playing along.

Helena then touches my clit softly with a tender amount of pressure, then she whispers against my ear, "And you're swollen too, my love."

Playfully, she asks, "How did you get this swollen, Alex?" As she rubs my clit with loving circles.

Giggling, I say, "Helena, you're not playing fair. Teasing me like this." She laughs and kisses me sweetly.

She pulls away and softly says, "I couldn't resist love. I won't tease you if you dislike it, darling."

"Oh, I didn't say I dislike it. It's actually driving me quite mad," I quickly confess. As Helena continues loving my clit she adds more pressure and gazes at me.

"Does this feel good, baby?" She asks sweetly.

Nodding, I say, "You have no idea; I'm having to hold back an orgasm. Loving you is where all my overabundant elixir is from, Miss Fitzgerald."

"It is, Miss Carrington?" She asks with that same seductive tone.

"Hmmmm," I moan into her ear, then add, "Yes, and you know it."

"Yes, I do, love. Do you remember when I told you I was going to devour you? Well, I am," she says as she moves to the side of the bed and then reaches for my hand. Grinning as I take her hand, our eyes lock, and I see my lovely Helena, wanting to please me, love me, and make me hers.

When I toss a pillow on the floor for her, she giggles and asks, "Is the pillow because of my age?" Then she laughs, getting me tickled.

"No, Helena! I just wanted to be thoughtful." We both laugh as we hug one another. "You're the one who is a damn knockout, Helena, and I would never know you're a day over forty."

"Nice try, my young one," she says with a chuckle. Sitting on the side of the bed with Helena on her knees, she wraps her arms around me and pulls me close. "I love you, Alex," she murmurs softly. Pulling away, she gazes at me, and I see her desire.

I kiss her lips, lean back onto my elbows, bring my legs up, and then open them for her. Helena massages my inner thighs and gazes at my womanness. "Alex, you're absolutely beautiful, love. My soul has ached to know your taste," she says softly as she kisses my thigh.

Watching Helena love me steals my breath. Our eyes merge, and I whisper, "I've wanted your perfect lips on me for so long, Helena."

"I must confess, Alex, since Savannah, I've thought of little else but how you would taste and smell, my love," Helena says softly before lowering her face to my sacred gateway. I feel her breathing me in. "Alex, you smell as if you did fall straight from heaven, my angel," she murmurs sweetly. She touches my folds opening them, and then gently places her mouth on my clit.

Helena wraps her arms around my thighs and then moves her tongue back and forth over my clit with the perfect amount of pressure. *How does she know how much pressure to give me?* I think as I watch her love me.

"Oh, Helena, your tongue feels so good on my clit, sweetheart," I faintly whisper. My heart and soul ache as Helena loves me. Breathlessly, I profess, "I've loved you for so long."

Helena looks up at me, moves her hand to my chest, then pushes me downward gently, as she seductively says, "Lie down, beautiful." With a grin, I submit to her request and close my eyes. As Helena continues loving me, she begins massaging my thighs as her tongue moves effortlessly across my clit.

Feeling my orgasm peak, I reach out my hands for hers. Helena immediately intertwines her fingers with mine. As I moan, my heart wants to explode along with my feminine soul. This woman—whom I've loved for so long—has me on the verge of release. My body tightens and all the beautiful fantasy I've ever had of her flood my mind. Breathlessly, I whisper, "Helena—my lovely Helena, I'm coming."

Grasping my hands tightly, she keeps the perfect pressure as if she's been my lover forever. Lifting my head, I gaze at her, our eyes lock, allowing her to see my vulnerability as I fall. This orgasm, so intense, filled with love, surges through me. Tears well in my midnight eyes—the ones she speaks of so often.

I moan loudly and cry out her beautiful name, "Helena—Helena." My orgasm continues as the tender pain rushes through me. The years of loving her silently have me gripped, and this orgasm is unyielding leaving only her sweet name on my lips.

As my orgasm softens, I see the love in her eyes, and my heart wants to weep. Closing my eyes, I lie back slowly against the bed and silently whisper, "Helena, please hold me?"

CHAPTER 11

HELENA

I move beside Alex and softly say, "Of course I'll hold you, baby." Gently pulling her warm, nude body against mine, I add, "I want to hold you in my arms forever." With her arms around my neck, I hold her close, my voice soft but firm as I whisper, "You're mine now, Alex, and I'll never let you go."

"Yes, I am definitely yours, Helena," she replies faintly, letting out a soft, comforting sigh as she relaxes into my embrace.

After I hold her for a while, my hand curves around her breast and I brush my thumb over her nipples; they peak immediately. Releasing her, I move back to my knees and pull her to me. As she sits on the edge of the bed, I hold her bosoms, then wink at her and say, "I'm not finished with you, Miss Carrington."

Alex gives me her bright laugh and hugs me as we both laugh. "You're not?" she asks with a chuckle, then gazes into my eyes and adds, "Yes, I can tell by the look in your eyes you're not done with me, Miss Fitzgerald."

"Damn, your bosoms are incredible, Alex," I say as I place

my mouth over one of her nipples and suck it tenderly, gazing into her eyes.

"Helena, that feels incredible."

As I continue sucking her nipples, my erotic desire for her builds with intense heat. While feeding on her breasts, Alex threads her fingers through my hair and pulls me into her, "Yes, Helena. Just like that baby," She coos.

With our eyes locked, I suck harder and watch the fire in Alex's midnight eyes begin to burn. "Yes, Helena, suck them, baby," she demands. Then, breathlessly adds, "Just like that, don't stop."

Locked in this erotic moment with Alex feels almost forbidden as I'm on my knees, pleasing her. Gazing at her, I can see she feels it too, "Yes, Helena, keep sucking my tits, and don't you stop until I tell you," She demands.

Sucking her tits as she demanded, I feel erotically seduced by this young vixen, and I have no problem with complying. I'll suck her tits as long as she asks me to. "Yes, baby. You love my tits, don't you?" She asks seductively. I wink slowly, and she immediately says, "You've got me on the verge of another orgasm, Helena."

With her fingers entangled in my hair, she pulls me away from her breasts and stands, then she looks down at me. As I gaze up at her, she says in a cool, demanding tone, "Go inside me, Helena." Reaching around her, I grasp her ass and then find her wetness. As I gaze up at her, I feel completely hypnotized by the allure of my lovely goddess, and all I want is to please her.

Pushing deeply into her, I watch her face and see the fire burning in those midnight gems. Alex pushes my face to her feminine mound, she says, "Fuck me, Helena." With my face pressed against her sex, I begin thrusting deeply into her. "Yes, baby, just like that," Alex says in a low sensual tone.

As I continue thrusting, I push my tongue against her clit

and begin loving it as before. "Yes, baby, you're fucking incredible, Helena." After a few strokes, I feel Alex begin to jerk slightly, and then she lets out an intense crying moan. Her fingers grip my hair, and she moans, "Helena!" As she keeps my head pressed against her sex.

When her orgasm ends, I stand and gaze into her fiery eyes, grab her, and pull her onto the bed beside me. I find her wetness, gather her elixir, and begin making firm circles on her clit. Alex stares into my soul, and then I watch her expression and feel her. She begins climaxing silently, but her eyes and body speak to me. "Yes, Alex, I feel you," I softly whisper as I watch her sultry gaze turn soft, and then she closes her sweet eyes.

Moving on top of Alex, she puts her arms around me tightly and pulls me close. Holding her quietly, I feel our intimate connection, and my soul wants to weep, rejoice, and completely surrender. "Was it good, baby?" I ask sweetly.

Alex doesn't speak for a moment, then quietly says, "You know it was, Helena. That time, I didn't just have an orgasm. You *were* my orgasm."

"Oh, Alex, my love. Like I told you before, you're mine now. I'm your home, and you're mine—do you understand?"

Alex pulls away and gazes into my eyes. "You're my home? Forever, Helena?"

Nodding at her, I whisper, "Yes, Alex. For as long as you want me."

She pulls me to her, and I feel her body relax and merge with mine. "I want you forever, Helena," she affirms as her fingers thread through my hair. Then she adds, "There could never be another woman for me."

Alex releases me, and I rise above her, gazing into her eyes. She murmurs, "Helena, I have no idea how we will make this work."

Smiling softly, I reply, "Neither do I, Alex, but you're what

I want more than anything in this world. I told you last night that you're everything I've ever wanted in a woman. And all I desire is to make you happy, Alex Carrington."

"Helena," she whispers.

I touch her lips tenderly, my eyes locked on her midnight gaze. "We'll make it work, Alex. The stars are already aligning for us as we speak, my love."

Suddenly, Alex grabs me, flipping us over as she laughs. "I love you, Helena Fitzgerald!" she exclaims boldly. I laugh with her, holding her cheeks in my hands as I look deeply into her sweet, tender soul. I know what I've found, and I'll never let her go.

❧

Sunday Evening

After handing my keys to the valet, a well-dressed man in a crisp uniform. I reach around Alex's waist and pull her close. "You look gorgeous, love. I wish I could hold your hand and kiss you right now," I say as I give her an intimate gaze.

Walking to the entrance of The Pump Room, Alex glances at me and whispers, "It's okay, sweetheart. I feel your hand in mine, and I know how your perfect lips taste."

Catching Alex's eyes I give her a tender smile and whisper, "I love you, woman."

Turning her lips to my ear she softly says, "And I love you." As we walk into the dining area of The Pump Room we are greeted with dim, intimate lighting from the many crystal chandeliers hanging above us. Crisp white linens cover the numerous tables. The reflection of the chandeliers sparkle against the wall of mirrors that help create a spacious and glamorous feel

Seated at a secluded corner table that I reserved days ago I turn my head and gaze at my beautiful date and I can't help but smile. The maître d' arrives with our champagne, opens it, then pours it delicately into the flutes.

After he leaves Alex grins and asks, "Are we celebrating tonight, Helena?"

"That depends on your answer, love. But even if the answer is no we will still be celebrating, Alex. Just being with you in a celebration.

"Oh, Helena," she whispers, then adds, "What do you need my answer to? Taking a deep breath I touch my champagne flute and gaze at it as I search for the right words.

Alex says, "Just ask me, Helena."

Glancing at my young love I see my future and know how beautiful it will be with this woman always beside me. "Alex, I love your vision and designs for *The Alex Collection* and want to help you if you will allow me to."

Alex smiles softly and asks, "In what way?"

With a nervous chuckle I say, "Well first I want to make a toast to *The Alex Collection*, may it bring you as much happiness as you've brought me Alex."

Touching our flutes together, Alex gazes deeply into my eyes and replies, "Helena, nothing could ever bring me the happiness that you have brought into my life. But tonight, we can definitely toast to *The Alex Collection*, sweetheart."

"Thank you for this lovely satin Emerald green dress, I love it. How did you know my size?" She asks with a tender laugh.

"It's my job, Alex. I knew your size the minute I laid eyes on you that day in the lounge of the hotel in Savannah," I say with a grin then add, "It looks beautiful on you, Alex. I knew the Emerald green would make your raven hair and midnight eyes shine even brighter."

Alex gives me a playful grin, sips her champagne then turns toward me and says, "Now ask me your real question, Helena."

Looking at her sweet face I say, "What would you say if I told you I wanted to leave Victor Voss and only remain as a consultant with them."

Giving me a surprised stare Alex says, "Darling, Victor Voss has been your whole life. Why would you ever think of leaving, especially now that you're the CCO?"

Finding Alex's hand beneath the table I secretly inter-twine her fingers with mine and say, "Alex do realize you asked and answered my question in the same sentence." Alex gives me a puzzled look, takes a sip of champagne then gazes back at me for more.

"Alex I love you and if you will allow me I would love to be your partner in life as well as your partner in *The Alex Collection*. You can design and have all the input you want and I'll be the Creative Director. I will oversee the artistic and branding aspects of the collection, collaborating closely with you to ensure that the brand always reflects your vision and designs."

Alex's eyes begin to sparkle as she gives me a broad smile nodding yes obviously unable to speak. I whisper, "I love you with everything in me, Alex."

After a moment Alex squeezes my hand and nods saying, "Helena, I can't believe how much you must love me. My god, you leaving Victor Voss for me is something I can't quite wrap my head around." She laughs and asks, "When did you think of this?"

About 3 A.M. this morning, but darling I've thought about your designs and how I could help you since the evening you showed your sketches to me in Savannah."

Alex reaches around me giving me a discreet hug, but whispers in my ear, "You're the love of my life, Helena Fitzgerald." Then she dabs a few tears with a handkerchief she pulled from her clutch.

"I feel the same way about you, Alex," she says seriously. "Darling, may I ask how much money you're investing into *The Alex Collection?*"

"Of course, Helena, you know most everything about me so sharing that tidbit of information is very small in comparison to what I've had to divulge about my life." She says with a soft gaze. Then adds, "Helena, I have Thirty-five-thousand dollars that I'm investing in the company. Why do you ask?"

"Because that's what I will invest as well and I want you to have 70% ownership and I'll have 30%. Is that alright with you, Alex?"

"Why wouldn't you ask for half ownership, Helena?"

Smiling, I say, "Because this is your vision, Alex. *The Alex Collection* was founded by you, love. And I never want you to feel as though I am taking anything from you, baby. Plus I'll still have a salary as a consultant with Victor Voss."

"Helena, with you as the creative director there is no way our company can fail," she says sincerely. Then adds, "And yes, I would love having you as my partner in life as well as our business. You make me so happy, Helena; happier than I've ever been."

I lift my flute and look at Alex and whisper, "To our beautiful life together, Alex."

She touches my flute with hers and says, "To our lives intertwined forever, Helena."

CHAPTER 12

ALEX

Two Weeks Later

Over the past two weeks, Helena and I have met with the Jewelry manufacturer, and they have completed the prototypes for *The Alex Collection.* I'm still in Chicago with Helena; the last couple of weeks with her have been magical.

We've made love every night and throughout our weekends. We've simply lived and breathed one another and *The Alex Collection.*

Today is Wednesday, the day before Thanksgiving. As I toss another log on the fire, I anticipate Helena's return home. This is her official last day with Victor Voss, and she is on her way back with our prototypes from *Artisan Jewel Craft,* our manufacturer.

As I wait for her to return home, I can't help but think about everything that's led to this point. Over the past year, each sketch I completed was just a dream. Now they're real—like everything between us.

Hearing the front door opening, I rush to Helena and

wrap my arms around her. She drops everything on the entryway floor, grasps me around my hips, and then picks me up giving me that charming smile that always melts me. "I love you, Alex," she exclaims.

"I love you, Helena, I still can't believe you're mine, sweetheart."

As she lowers me to the floor, she sweetly replies, "I know what I'm thankful for this Thanksgiving, Alex. Loving you has brought my world to life."

Hugging her, I snuggle into the crook of her neck and sigh, then whisper, "Do you have them?"

Helena pulls away and teasingly asks, "Have what, love?" Then she laughs and says, "Yes, I have them, baby. Come on, let's look at them."

"You didn't glance at them, Helena?"

"Of course I didn't. These are your designs, so I couldn't look at them without you, Alex."

Laying the gold and silver bracelets and brooches out on Helena's dining table, I'm too emotional to speak. My designs, the ones I've spent the last year sketching and pouring my heart into, are absolutely breathtaking. "Helena," I whisper.

Looking at them, I realize they're much more than just jewelry—they're pieces of my soul, made of gold and silver. I run my fingers over one, tracing the lines, the aquamarines, and I feel Helena's warm and loving gaze on me, grounding me in this moment.

Helena pulls me to her and threads her fingers through my hair. "You should be very proud, Alex. These are the most beautiful bracelets and brooches I've ever seen," She says as she releases me and then touches my cheek, brushing my jaw gently with her thumb.

Gazing back at the jewelry, I smile and clasp my hands together. "Helena, look what we've done, baby."

"This is mainly you, Alex, but I've been working on our branding. Growing The Alex Collection will be my main focus as soon as we approve these prototypes and make our initial order."

"Do you love them, Helena?" I ask as I gaze at the aqua-marines set against the luster of the gold and silver.

Encircling me from behind Helena leans over my shoulder and continues peering at the sparking bracelets and brooches with me. "They're designed from your heart, Alex. How could I help but be in love with them? You've created something extraordinary. It's not just the designs; it's the heart you put into them. I can see your love in these pieces, just like I see it in us."

Alex turns toward me and reaches around my neck, offering her full body for me to love. I embrace her and she whispers, "I'm hungry."

Laughing, Alex releases me and takes off, running up the stairs as I chase her. I join her in laughter all the way to the bedroom. Then I grab her and pull her to the bed as she giggles. "I've missed you today," she says as we lie beside one another.

"Why don't you show me how much you missed me?" Helena asks seductively as she moves on top of me.

Threading my fingers through her hair, I grin, gaze into those steel-blue eyes I fell for years ago, and whisper gently, "Yes, I believe I will, Miss Fitzgerald."

∾

Monday after Thanksgiving

Helena and I went to The Pump Room for our Thanksgiving Dinner. We realized early on that we have one thing in common: neither of us likes to cook.

It's Monday now. We caught a morning flight to Chattanooga, picked up my car at the train depot, and now we're roaring up a back road outside the city in my MG Roadster.

Taking a minute from time to time to glance at Helena I want to burst with laughter. It's obvious this woman hasn't seen the countryside in years. "What are those, Alex?" She asks, pointing to a structure with fencing around it.

Chucking I say, "Those are chicken coops. They house several chickens and the fencing around it is so the chicks can graze and roam freely, but also stay protected."

"Do you have chickens?" She asks with a chuckle.

"Yes, remember I told you about the chickens and Bessie on one of our first telephone calls." I say as I laugh into her beautiful eyes.

"Oh hush! You're as much a city girl as I am. I bet other than your charming farmhouse there isn't one thing on your property that screams, 'I'm a country-girl.'"

"Well, I must admit, you're right about that. Even my neighbors don't know what to make of me especially when I zoom past them in this car."

Helena laughs loudly and says, "I wonder what they will think of you bringing a woman home with you?"

Shaking my head I glance at Helena and say, "Maybe we better get some chickens." We both roar with laughter as the Roadster zips up the last road that reaches the farmhouse. "This road is called *Carrington Holler.* This is the road my home is on, sweetheart."

"What's a holler? What does that mean?" Helena asks with a straight face.

Stopping the car, I roar with laughter, my head falling

backward as I clutch my tummy. Helena joins in my laughter as she gazes at me shaking her head.

Putting the car back in gear I take off up *Carrington Holler* once again. Then say, "A holler is a small valley. You see that mountain? I ask as I point upward.

"Yes, that's indeed a mountain," Helena says with a chuckle.

"That's Lookout Mountain, and over there is Signal Mountain. Down below, where I live, is the valley. Most country folks call it a holler, but I just call it the valley."

"Is that because you aren't truly a country girl, Miss Carrington?"

"Perhaps, but I just like the word valley better," I reply as I turn onto the long drive that will take us to the farmhouse. "We're home, sweetheart."

"We are? Where's the house?" Helena quickly asks.

Laughing I say, "We will be there in a moment darling, this is my long driveway. The house is located away from the road."

"Well, I won't even ask why," Helena says with a chuckle. I'm clearly in unfamiliar territory." She gazes at me with an anxious stare and adds, "Please tell me you have indoor plumbing and electricity, Alex."

With a straight face that wants to burst with laughter I say, "No, darling, but they say by next winter it should be out this way."

"Alex! Seriously?!

Laughing I say, "I just bathe in the creek, darling." Then I glance at her and wink.

"Oh god, Alex. Well, I think you're pulling my leg, but I'd live with you regardless." The late afternoon sun sets as we slowly approach the farmhouse, casting a golden light on the other love of my life—this home. A gift from my loving grandmother passed down to me when she left this world over two years ago.

"My gosh, Alex, this is beautiful, baby. What a grand farmhouse this is. No wonder you wanted to move here," Helena says as I halt the Roadster at the end of the drive. Meeting her gaze, she seductively adds, "I can't wait to make love to you in that charming farmhouse, Alex Carrington, who lives on *Carrington Holler.*"

Grinning, I lean over and kiss her perfect lips, then say excitedly, "Come on, sweetheart, let's go inside." Removing our luggage from the leather straps on the back of the Roadster, we walk across the yard and step up onto the porch..

"My God, relaxing in this huge clawfoot tub with you, full of warm water after this long day, is amazing. And you, my love, are very fetching, Miss Carrington."

"Fetching? Well, Miss Fitzgerald, you do know a few country words after all."

Helena chuckles and says, "Look at me, I haven't even been here twenty-four hours, and I'm already speaking the language." We both laugh, and then I get on my knees, grasp the sides of the tub, and playfully present my bosoms in front of Helena.

"Yes, Miss Carrington? Would you like for me to suck those beautiful tits of yours?"

"Oh God, Helena, you make me crazy when you call them that," I say, giggling as I fall softly against her.

"Come here, baby, I'll take care of you," she says seductively then begins sucking my nipples. "You like this, lover?" She asks playfully.

"Helena, I'm going to orgasm in about fifteen seconds." After I say this, Helena moves her fingers to my clit, applying the perfect pressure like she always does. As I watch her suck my nipples, I feel my orgasm rising. "Yes, baby, suck my tits like you love to do."

Grabbing me forcefully, Helena grips me around my waist, pulling my breasts against her as she continues to love me. Threading my fingers through her hair, I surrender completely, letting go and singing her name, just as I always do when I'm orgasming. "Helena—Helena."

CHAPTER 13

HELENA

Christmas Eve in Chattanooga

It's Christmas Eve, and I can't remember the last time I had this much time off or felt so alive. Over the past three weeks, Alex and I have embraced a simple life, loving one another and eagerly awaiting Christmas much like children. As we sit by the fire, I gaze at her—my beautiful young woman—watching the glow of the flames warm her face.

"I love you, Alex," I whisper softly.

Alex turns toward me, and our eyes lock; neither can speak. She reaches for my hand, grasping it gently as she whispers, "Helena, you make me feel more like a woman than I've ever felt in my life. How you love me, make love to me, and treat me is unlike anything I've ever known."

Pulling her closer, I kiss her cheek and say, "That makes me so happy. Knowing you feel that way with me means everything. You're every bit a woman, Alex—a passionate, hot-blooded woman who's shown me what true passion and love are. I'm deeply in love with you."

Alex slowly shakes her head, whispering, "I wanted you so badly back then, Helena." She turns her gaze back to the firelight and adds, "But I'm glad it didn't happen until now. I'm old enough to love you like a woman and truly appreciate you as one."

"You treat me like one, Alex. And you definitely make me feel like a woman," I say as I gaze at her. Glancing at our beautiful Christmas tree, I add, "That's the most beautiful and genuine tree I've ever known. I can't believe you and I actually went into the woods and chopped it down ourselves," I say, shaking my head and giggling.

Standing, I walk over to the tree and pick up the Christmas gift I have for Alex. Then I sit beside her again. Handing it to her, I say, "Merry Christmas, my love."

Alex gazes at the box for a moment, then lifts her eyes, meeting mine. She gives me a playful grin as she shakes the box. "What's in this tiny box, Helena?"

"My commitment to you, Alex." Giving me a perplexed look, she removes the delicate bow and then unwraps it slowly. As I continue watching the warm glow of the firelight illuminate her lovely face, I feel my heart and soul expand with love.

Opening the ring box, she softly exclaims, "Helena, this is absolutely beautiful, sweetheart." Tears well in her midnight eyes, glistening in the firelight. Alex looks at me, shaking her head slowly, and adds, "Not in a million years would I have ever guessed that I would have you loving me like this or that you would give me this gorgeous ring on Christmas Eve."

Moving close to her, I kiss her cheek and softly ask, "Do you like it, Alex?"

Shaking her head slowly, she gently touches my cheeks and pulls me in for a tender kiss—a slow, lingering kiss that aches beautifully in my soul. Gazing into her eyes, I say, "It's an Asscher cut, and I chose the special aquamarine myself, then had the jeweler add the diamonds."

"Helena," she whispers softly, then hands the box back to me. Seeing the confusion on my face, she chuckles and asks, "Will you put it on my finger for me, sweetheart?"

Smiling into her dark eyes, I nod and whisper, "Yes, Alex." As I place the ring on her wedding ring finger, I lift my gaze to hers and add, "This officially means you belong to me, Alex Carrington. Now and forever."

Rising to her knees, Alex offers her body to me, inviting my embrace. Pulling her warmth against me, I take a moment to truly feel the contours of her womanly form as I hold her in my arms. "I love you, Helena," she whispers.

Pulling away, she gazes into my eyes and smiles sweetly. She rises and retrieves a gift beneath our wonderful Christmas tree. Sitting beside me, she whispers, "This is my commitment to you, Helena Fitzgerald."

With a broad smile, I unwrap a gift of the same size I gave her. As I slowly open the ring box, I softly say, "Alex, my love." Gazing at the stunning aquamarine ring, I can't help but laugh. Lifting my eyes to her, I add, "This is the most beautiful ring I've ever seen, love. Please place it on my finger."

Alex gently slides the ring onto my wedding finger, holding my hand as she gazes at me and softly says, "Helena, before our worlds collided, I felt unworthy of anything good. But your love saved me. Loving you has made me realize I have much to offer and deserve anything I wish for. And you, Helena Fitzgerald, have always been my biggest wish."

"Oh, Alex, my love. You have such a pure and tender heart. I couldn't help but fall for you," I whisper against her lips, then kiss them softly. After our kiss, Alex rises, walks to the phonograph, and puts on a Christmas tune.

She walks back to me and extends her hand. Rising, I

smile and pull her close. She gently asks, "Do you remember?"

Holding her tight, I whisper, "Yes, I remember that sweet telephone call, Alex. I believe you said, 'Maybe we can dance together sometime,' I responded that I loved that idea, especially to a very slow song."

"I thought it was very fitting to play *The Christmas Song* by Ella Fitzgerald for my own Miss Fitzgerald," she says with a giggle, then smiles into my eyes. As we dance, our eyes lock, and I gaze at the catchlights from the firelight in her midnight eyes.

"Merry Christmas, Alex," I say, holding her gaze.

Alex leans in and kisses my lips. Her kiss is delicate and tender, reminding me of our first kiss in Savannah—the magical kiss that dissolved everything around us except for the softness between us. As she breaks our tender kiss, Alex whispers against my lips, "Merry Christmas, Helena."

EPILOGUE

Three Months later: March 1950
Chicago
Alex

"Good morning, sexy," I whisper seductively into Helena's ear. She giggles, playfully shifting her weight and moving onto me. As I smile into her steel-blue eyes, I thread my fingers through her soft locks of blonde hair. "My god, you're so gorgeous!" I exclaim.

She giggles again and replies, "Call me vain, but I never tire of your flattery, Alex." Her strong hand runs down my body, massaging every muscle in her path. "You feel delicious," she adds with a sultry tone.

"Delicious?" I chuckle.

"Yes, incredibly delicious," she murmurs, her voice low and inviting.

"Helena, you feel incredible, but I don't think we have time. It's already 7:30," I say, feeling somewhat deflated.

"I don't have time for just one taste?" she purrs.

"Woman, you have me on edge. Do you realize I can practically orgasm from just the sound of your voice? My god, the control you have over me is unreal," I admit, pulling her closer and whispering, "Tonight?"

Nodding, she smiles and says, "Well, we just learned a very sobering fact about working for ourselves. We can't call in sick to stay home and fuck all day," She says with a chuckle and her eyes sparkling.

"Helena, you're awful," I laugh as I rise from the bed. "I'll go make coffee. If you want to shower first."

With Helena still wrapped beautifully in the sheets, she gazes at me, then says, "Go start the coffee, love, and then join me in the shower."

After starting the percolator, I rush back upstairs and step into the warm shower with my love. "Come here, Alex," she softly says, pulling me closer. As she bathes me, I completely submit to her loving touch. "Does this feel good, love?" she asks, her hands gliding over my skin.

Faintly, I whisper, "Yes, you know how you affect me, Helena."

"Yes, I do, love. And I think it's beautiful when you submit to me like this. You must truly feel safe with me, Alex."

"I know I'm safe with you, Helena. I've felt that with you from day one."

~

After we park Helena's Cadillac, we walk up Michigan Avenue to our Jewelry Boutique, *The Alex Collection*, located on the Magnificent Mile. "Look at that beautiful sign, my love," Helena says with heightened enthusiasm as she loops her arm through mine. Then she adds, "I love seeing your name up there, Alex."

Smiling at her I reply, "Helena, none of this would be possible had you not joined me in this venture. I know I would have made it eventually, but it would have taken much longer without you, sweetheart."

"Oh, Alex, perhaps. But none of this would have ever happened without your vision and the love you've poured into this. And I would still be at Victor Voss, enjoying it but not in love with it as I am with our company and you, Alex."

Walking into the boutique, I return the burglar alarm lever to the off position, and Helena begins flipping on the light switches. The beautiful Crystal chandeliers and wall sconces illuminate the small boutique, creating a luxurious feel.

Smiling at Helena, I say, "This is my favorite part of the opening when you turn on our lighting. It's as if our shop comes to life saying, Good Morning, it's time to make our customers happy,"

Helena winks at me and replies, "It's a beautiful and happy shop, Alex, but this is just a stepping stone for where we are taking *The Alex Collection*, my love." She walks over, touches my back, and says, "Look at all these beautiful bracelets and brooches you've created, my love."

Nodding, I kiss her cheek and say, "I'm so very happy with where we are. I know you and I will make it grand, but I want us to enjoy every step of this journey, Helena."

She replies, "You're right, Alex. I've been in a world where growth was most important. I suppose now I'll need to learn how to slow down and enjoy every step, as you said. Hopefully, with you holding my hand, I can learn that."

Helena smiles, winks at me, and nods, and says, "Will you meet me in our office for a moment, Miss Carrington?"

Giving her an intense gaze, I playfully reply, "Yes, Miss Fitzgerald, I'll be right there." As I walk into our small office, Helena grabs me, and I giggle. "Yes, what did you need, ma'am?" I ask playfully.

As she pulls me close, she looks at my breasts and seductively asks, "Well, I was wondering if you and these bosoms I crave so much would take me to Chattanooga this weekend?"

"What's in Chattanooga, Miss Fitzgerald?" I ask seductively.

"Well, if I remember correctly, there is a big clawfoot tub full of warm water that I would love to seduce you in. I mean, that is if you're willing to take me." She asks seriously.

Gazing into Helena's eyes, I reach around and grasp her ass, replying, "Tell you what. If you're a good girl and get all your work done this week, I'll take you to Chattanooga, and you can do anything you want with me, and to me." I then lick her lips, exit the office, and walk back into the showroom.

The twinkle of the entry door goes off, and a nice-looking older woman walks in smiling. I warmly say, "Good morning, welcome to *The Alex Collection*."

∾

The Weekend in Chattanooga

As Helena and I zip back up *Carrington Hollow*, she glances at me and says, "If someone had told me a year ago I'd crave the countryside like this, I would've said they clearly didn't know me."

Laughing, I reply, "Now look at you, practically a local."

"Well, I wouldn't go that far, Alex. We haven't even bought those chickens yet," she teases. I laugh, glancing over to see the happiness lighting up her face.

Once inside the farmhouse, I reach around her, grab her hips, and lift her up. "We're home, sweetheart. Now go turn on that hot water, woman," I demand playfully as I set her down and give her a quick swat on the ass.

"Alex! You naughty girl," she calls back, grinning as she

heads toward the bathroom. As I hear the water running, I pull out my Billie Holiday record and place it on the phonograph. For a brief moment, memories of young Alex flood my mind, and I can't help but smile.

As Miss Holiday begins singing *The Very Thought of You,* I dance all the way into the bathroom and then keep dancing —very badly—for Miss Fitzgerald. As she laughs, I do a striptease for her, taking off one garment at a time, very slowly, while she continues to giggle.

Stepping into the warm water, I ease myself down onto Helena's lap and giggle with her. "God, how I love you, Alex Carrington. These past few months have been so joyful with you, darling," she says with a huge grin.

Wrapping my arms around her neck, I melt against her warm, wet curves and relax. Pulling back just enough to gaze into those beautiful eyes, I whisper, "And I love you, Helena Fitzgerald." Then, I lay my head against her neck, listening to the sounds of the music that sixteen-year-old Alex loved, feeling as safe as she once did—safe once again.

THANK YOU

Thank you for reading *Romancing Miss Fitzgerald*. I hope you enjoyed it!
I'd love it if you would take a moment to leave a review on Amazon and share your thoughts. Your feedback would mean so much to me!
Aven

ALSO BY AVEN BLAIR

ABOUT THE AUTHOR

Aven is a devoted author of age-gap sapphic lesbian romances, celebrated for her sweet yet fiery love stories that always promise a happily ever after. Writing from her quaint Southern town, she crafts captivating narratives centered around strong Southern women as they navigate love and life in historical settings. With a blend of warmth, humor, and emotional depth, Aven's stories enchant readers with unforgettable romances and her unwavering commitment to love in all its forms.

Printed in Great Britain
by Amazon

54175347R00061